# The Unexpected War

# The Unexpected War

*life after death*

## Jean-Pierre Breton

iUniverse, Inc.
Bloomington

# THE UNEXPECTED WAR
# LIFE AFTER DEATH

*iUniverse books may be ordered through booksellers or by contacting:*

*iUniverse*
*1663 Liberty Drive*
*Bloomington, IN 47403*
*www.iuniverse.com*
*1-800-Authors (1-800-288-4677)*

*Because of the dynamic nature of the Internet, any web addresses or links contained in this book may have changed since publication and may no longer be valid. The views expressed in this work are solely those of the author and do not necessarily reflect the views of the publisher, and the publisher hereby disclaims any responsibility for them.*

*Any people depicted in stock imagery provided by Thinkstock are models, and such images are being used for illustrative purposes only.*

*Certain stock imagery © Thinkstock.*

*ISBN: 978-1-4759-8312-8 (sc)*
*ISBN: 978-1-4759-8313-5 (hc)*
*ISBN: 978-1-4759-8314-2 (e)*

*Library of Congress Control Number: 2013905373*

*Printed in the United States of America*

*iUniverse rev. date: 3/25/2013*

# CHAPTER 1

SUNDAY MORNING OF AUGUST 17, 2032, started out like every other one—an average, mediocre, not-too-great but not-too-shabby kind of day. It had been only two days ago that Kate had burst through the door with a huge smile across her face informing us that we were going camping. Tina and I rarely agreed with one another about anything, but we both shared that same look of disgust knowing it was going to be a long weekend.

Alas, it was finally over, though. After two dreary days stuck under the foot of a towering cave with nothing to keep us company but the dull pitter-patter of the rain outside, our nightmare was drawing to an end. Well, at least that's what I had thought.

"Lance, leave your sister alone!" The angry yell echoed around the cave.

"But, Kate, she started it!" I accused, pointing to Tina.

"Shut up. You did!" Tina shot back, wiping the dirt off her pants.

"Just drop it. For God's sake, you two are thirteen. Stop acting like children," Kate scolded us.

The stern glare that followed was enough to shatter

rock. Kate wasn't always like this; she used to be fun and bouncy, always seen with a smile on her face or a treat in her pocket. Ever sense our mother had passed away, though, there was so much of a burden on her that she was forced to grow up quickly for both Tina and I.

Kate gave her long, wavy dark hair a pat and then returned to packing; seeming content that she had silenced us—at least for now. "I didn't even want to go on this stupid camping trip anyway," I muttered, kicking the ground in anger.

A rock rolled across the cave and hit Tina's leg unintentionally. She glared over at me, folding her arms across her chest. "When are we going home?" She complained, directing the anger elsewhere.

"When all this is packed and ready to go," Kate called over to Tina, who was now moping around the cave while fiddling with a package of batteries.

Inspired by the hope of getting out of the damp, musty cave, I began to help Kate take down the tent. "You fighting with your brother isn't going to make this move along any faster," Kate reminded Tina, siding with me for once.

Tina gave Kate a saucy roll of the eyes before returning her attention back to fiddling with the batteries. By midday, everything was packed and ready to go. I grabbed my father's hunting rifle that was leaning up against the edge of the cave and shouldered it with a sling.

We then began the journey along an overgrown path that would lead us back toward our house in Dublin, accompanied only by the dull drizzle the day had to offer. "When we get home, can Lucy and Danielle come over?" Tina asked.

"Yes, as long as they don't bother your brother," Kate told her.

I let out an angry sigh as I readjusted the straps on my backpack; those three not bothering me would never happen. As a matter of fact, I was convinced that their sole mission in life was to annoy me. After walking along the path for a few more minutes in silence, I saw something out of the corner of my eye that caught my attention.

Thunder boomed out above us; the sky lit up with a blinding white light. I gasped in disbelief, frozen in place as huge boulders of fire streaked like meteors towards the earth. The faint sounds of explosions coming from Dublin far off in the distance could already be heard.

"What's happening?" Tina whispered to herself in a trance, staring up at the sky, which seemed to have millions of the fireballs raining down from it now.

Kate didn't answer; she looked just as stunned as we were, her mouth wide open. Our awe soon began to develop into panic, though. "Quick! Back to the cave, you two," Kate said, placing her hands on our backs and pushing us up the path toward the cave we had just come from.

Tina let out a scream as one of the meteorites came crashing through the tree line off to our right, smashing into the earth about a hundred meters away spraying us with dirt and vegetation. "Hurry, run!" Kate yelled as the forest around us seemed to erupt into flame.

We didn't need to be told twice. Throwing the camping gear to the ground, we took off sprinting up the same overgrown path we had just come down from. Once we were in the safety of the cave, we watched in awe as the relentless barrage of fireballs came crashing down into the forest around us, causing massive explosions everywhere.

With each fireball that smashed into the forest, the ground below us would tremble uncontrollably. One of them hit the ground right below the cave we were taking shelter in enveloping the area in smoke. Once it began to clear, we could make out a metal ball about ten feet around resting in the dirt crater it had created.

A side door opened, and more smoke billowed out. To our shock, a human emerged from it. "Get down," Kate whispered, but Tina and I were already flat against the rocky surface of the cave, holding our breath.

The creature looked up to the sky, a smile spreading across his face. Then, without warning, he let out an angry, lionlike roar. His muscles went into a spasm as his skin faded away, replaced with a hard, reptile-looking skin and black fur that sprouted out all across his body. His fingernails turned into daggerlike fingers as the hands transformed into paws similar to a bear's.

He dropped to all fours, his face turning into something resembling a saber-toothed tiger. Wings protruded from his sides, completing the transformation. The creature let out a gut-wrenching roar as it stood up on its hind legs; the call was returned by another creature's roar off in the distance.

Without hesitation the creature then launched itself into the air through the tree line and into the sky, streaking toward Dublin. I felt a nudge against my side. I glanced over to see Tina staring at me. "Did you see that?" she whispered, trembling uncontrollably.

"Are you stupid? Of course I did."

"Cut it out," Kate whispered.

We both did, obediently lying flat against the rocky surface of the cave as more creatures began to fly by. A few hours past before Kate mustered up the courage to dig through her bag opening a can of kippers for us. I couldn't help noticing her hand shaking.

The three of us split it. I kind of felt bad for snapping at Tina now as I glanced over at her. She was still trembling. Kate took on a motherly role, allowing Tina to rest against her stomach as she stroked her naturally curly blonde hair.

A few more hours passed, and then they fell asleep. With a glance to the foot of the cave, I could see that dusk was setting in outside. After waiting a few more minutes in silence, satisfied by the dull snoring of Kate, I knew it was the perfect time to go explore the now very unfamiliar world around us.

Silently as I could, I reached for my timber wolf hunting rifle and then climbed down the entrance of the cave to the rocky dirt path below. "Where are you going?" I heard the urgent whisper come from behind me.

I glanced back up to the entrance of the cave; Tina was staring down at me. "Go back to sleep; stop being a pest," I called up to her.

An angry sigh was all I could summon as Tina ignored me like usual and scrambled down the front of the cave, coming to a rest by my side. "Why do you always have to be such a pain?" I asked her through clenched teeth. She ignored me; I angrily turned on my heels, slinging the hunting rifle over my shoulder, and headed toward Dublin.

"What do you think them things are?" she asked, peeking through the leaves of the trees above as the aliens continued to fly by overhead.

"I don't know. They're definitely not human." was all I could come up with.

As we advanced closer to the city, the smell of smoke became more and more pungent, surrounding the air around us. The two of us began cresting a small hill, revealing the towering, now-burning skyscrapers of Dublin. We found shelter in a few shrubs and then peeked out at the carnage below through the safety of the thick vegetation's leaves.

There were burning cars, dead bodies, and craters littering the street below where a local market of shops and a Quick Stop gas station once stood.

"Help!" someone cried out in distress.

I spotted the man limping out of the burning Quick Stop. I was about to stand up and wave my arms to him but Tina grabbed my shirt, keeping me down.

"What are you doing?" I whispered to her, confused.

She pointed through the smoke where I could make out four glowing red eyes tucked away in an alley. They appeared to be focused on the man in front of us crying for help. "What are they doing?" she whispered.

"I think they're using him as bait," I replied.

Tina gave me a questioning look. "They want us to go out and help him so they can kill us," I explained to her.

She gulped, nodding as we lowered closer down into the grass. We both watched the injured man try to limp away to safety from the raging flames of the building he had just escaped from. Sure enough, not even a moment passed by before a Good Samaritan came out from the ruble of another building to help the man. This act of kindness was greeted by the sound of gunfire filling the cool night air.

The two humans slumped to the ground, probably

dead before they even knew what happened. "Monsters," I growled in disgust.

Two creatures emerged from the alley they had been taking cover in and began to slash open and eat their kills as we watched in horror. "Don't look, Tina. It's okay; just don't look. Everything's going to be fine." I tried to console her by patting her hair as she cried silently into her arms.

When the two creatures finished feasting on the dead bodies, they bit into the legs of the completely disfigured humans and dragged them into the alley. A second later, they exited in human form. One of them sat down clutching his stomach and pretending to be hurt as the female one took a bloody rag and pressed it against his stomach to make it look realistic.

"*Help*! Somebody help me! My father's been shot!" She began screaming.

"I'll help you," I muttered to myself as I set up the stand of the hunting rifle. My targets appeared to be about four hundred meters away.

I adjusted my scope's elevation and then took a deep breath, calming myself down as I took aim before firing the shot. It found its mark; the female alien was killed instantly, falling into the other alien's lap. The creature stared at her in shock and then let out an angry snarl searching for me. He looked in my direction before scrambling for cover; he wasn't fast enough to escape my second shot, which sailed right through his head. He fell, joining the female in a pool of their purplish blood.

Tina gasped, staring at the two creatures in disbelief. "You killed them?"

I glanced over to her and gave an unsure nod. "I think so."

"No, wait. What are you doing, Lance?" She yelled to me as I got to my knee and stared through my scope, searching for any more enemies.

"Stay here," I ordered her.

She stared at me for a second and then nodded her obedience. I couldn't help letting out an inward smile. This would probably be the first and last time that she would ever listen to me for the remainder of my life. I jogged down to the bodies of the dead creatures, slowing down to a trot as I reached them.

The second monster who I had shot through its head was gurgling as purple blood oozed from the bullet hole. I reached into the pocket of the dead female and pulled out a man-made pistol. I cocked the gun then aimed at the gurgling alien, mercilessly firing three shots into its chest to end what little life he had left in him. I reached into his pocket and pulled out a note and another handgun.

Quickly looking around, I opened the note in an attempt to read it, but it was all in writing and symbols that I had never seen before. Shouldering my rifle, I kept the pistol by my side as I walked the short distance to the alleyway the fiends had been taking refuge in. "Oh God," I gasped. The stench was unbearable.

There were six or seven dead human bodies piled on top of each other at the end of the alley. Along the wall sat two backpacks and a pair of bulletproof vests. Leaning against the gear were two assault rifles.

I gathered all the equipment, knowing it would come in handy later down the road and then ran back through the ruble into the woods where I had left Tina. "Tina?" I called timidly.

"Over here," she called back.

I followed her voice and eventually found her hidden by a bush. To my surprise, there was another girl beside her who appeared to be the same age as us. "Who are you?" I asked while handing a bag, the vest, and assault rifle to Tina.

"My name is Rachel," she whispered.

The girl's hair was a mess, laced with the dust and dirt off the destroyed buildings. I could see the fright in her eyes; Tina was begging me to take her with us. I sighed, nodding for Rachel to follow us. I handed her the other assault rifle after loading it.

"Put that vest on," I ordered Tina, who did so obediently.

I handed Rachel mine. She smiled, thanking me as she put it on. It took us about twenty minutes to reach the safety of the cave.

To my shock, it was now filled with twenty-five to thirty masked men with guns smoking and joking amongst themselves. Across from the rebels were about fifteen women and children sitting along the wall of the cave. The only conclusion that I could come to was that these people must have been some of the survivors from Dublin.

Kate could be seen pacing back and forth. All attention shifted to us as Rachel, Tina, and I stood at the foot of the cave not knowing what to do. "Were did you two go?!" Kate exclaimed, her voice a mixture of joy and anger.

She ran over to Tina and me wrapping her arms around the both of us. "Dublin," I admitted.

Kate slapped me across the face. "*What were you thinking, Lance Andrew Burns?!*"

I nursed the cheek apologetically staring at her knowing I was in big trouble; she never used my three names in the same sentence unless I was in for it. All I could offer was a meek shrug followed by a timid, "Sorry, Kate."

I could tell she was about to continue yelling but then she spotted the extra weapons and equipment we had brought back with us. "Where did you get those guns from?" she questioned.

"Lance killed two of the monsters with Dad's hunting rifle!" Tina blurted out.

"Thanks a lot, Tina!" I muttered, giving her a punch to the shoulder.

"Ouch!" she cried.

Before Kate could resume yelling at me, one of the masked gunmen got between us. "That's enough," he ordered Kate. "Please remove those flak jackets, ladies," he added, taking the two assault rifles from Rachel and Tina.

"Wait! That's for my sister!" I objected as one of the masked men helped remove the flak jacket she was wearing.

"Sorry, kid, everything goes to the resistance. We can't fight these things with rocks," one of them told me.

A soldier came over, extending his hand to me. I stared at it, confused. "The backpack," he grunted.

"Oh," I muttered, unstrapping and then handing him the bag filled with supplies.

He tried to take my timber wolf, but I backed away from him defiantly. It had been a gift from my father; no one was going to take that away from me. Another man appeared from behind him and patted the soldier's shoulder, causing him to back off. The second man asked Tina, Kate, and the new girl we had found at Dublin to go join the others.

As he took off his mask, I could see that he was an older

gentleman in his early forties, about six feet tall, his hair already graying. "So you killed two fiends, eh?" he asked.

"Fiends? Is that what they're called?" I questioned him.

He laughed with a shrug. "They're monsters, not humans. Could you think of a better word to describe them?"

"No," I muttered, feeling foolish for asking.

He smiled and gave me a wink, which made me feel better. "So you killed two of them?"

"Yes, sir," I said. My voice was quivering a little, but I tried to stand up straight as if I wasn't afraid of the man's presence.

"What is your name son?"

"Lance."

He paused, debating something as he gnawed on a toothpick staring at me. "Would you like to join the People's Liberation Force?" He offered.

"The People's Liberation Force?" I asked, confused.

He nodded. "We're a small group of Canadian soldiers. The army has been disbanded; we need to stop these things from killing the innocent. The only way to do that is by forming a rebellion against these fiends. We can't win this war on our own, son. We need people like you."

"My sister would never allow it," I replied, blushing in embarrassment.

The man squatted down staring into my eyes, "Forget your sister. This is a grown man's decision.... Are you a man?" he asked.

"Yes, sir," I replied, straightening up.

"Then what do you say, boy?"

I paused. "Okay, on one condition sir."

"What is that?" He asked.

"I keep my timber wolf."

The man extended his hand to me. I did the same, nerves griping my stomach as his hand grasped mien giving it a firm shake. "We have a deal my boy, welcome to the war."

I gulped. Staring at my hand as the blood returned to it. "Tha...Thank you sir." I stammered.

He stood up placing his hand on my shoulder leading me into the cave, "There is no need to be scared Lance this war will be over before you know it."

If only we both knew how wrong he would be.

# Chapter 2

A FTER THE INVASION, MY sisters and I, along with survivors from Dublin, were lead by the PLF deep into the heart of the Harush Forest. The going was rough; it took days. Not everyone was in as good of shape as the rebels, so we had to take many breaks—not to mention the late August nights were nothing short of bitter cold. Arriving to our final destination we came to a rest along a flat piece of land with plenty of trees that would provide overhead protection from rain and enemy patrols.

I glanced around the area, taking in the scenery. It looked like a great place to set up camp. There was a hill leading up to a den tucked away in a rocky cliff, not to mention lots of flat area to build our shelters on.

Kate and Tina were sitting on the ground behind the group; they hadn't spoken to me since my decision to join the People's Liberation Force, but I hoped they would forgive me. "I'm sorry, Kate," I said as I timidly approached them.

They both looked up at me. A tear ran down Kate's cheek, and she just nodded her head patting the grass beside her, gesturing for me to sit down. I did, and we shared a can of tuna between the three of us as the shadows of the trees began to creep around the meadow, signaling the end of yet another long day.

"Harrumph," the grunt of the leader's voice sounded.

I glanced over at the man who had asked me to join the resistance. He stood perched on a fallen tree with a few armed men around him. He smiled reassuringly to all of us as everyone's attention shifted to him. "Greetings, my name is Captain Murphy. My men and I will do everything in our power to protect you as we work through this disaster together. The first priority is reconstructing the lives we have all lost. It is going to be dark soon so ill keep this brief in order for everyone to get a good start on their shelter. Starting tomorrow, we will begin building a camp, all will be welcome, soldier or not. My hope is that life over time will return to somewhat normal for all of us. Thank you for your time." When he was done speaking, he stepped down. A wave of timid claps followed him.

Tina, Kate, and I all glanced at each other. "We should probably start the shelter," Tina whispered.

Kate and I nodded in agreement. We only had about forty-five minutes before sundown, but by the time the last of the light was slipping through the treetops, we had constructed a small lean-to out of sticks, logs, and fallen pine tree branches to shield us from the weather that the night would surely bring. It looked like the shelter was too small for the three of us, so I took it upon myself to lie out a bit farther, letting Tina and Kate inside. I shivered from the full brunt of the wind as my sisters huddled with one another under an old blanket in the shelter.

"Come here, Lance," I heard Kate's soft, caring voice call to me.

I glanced at her and Tina shivering beneath the shelter before obediently squeezing myself in with them. They placed their hands against my back as the three of us huddled together, sharing our body heat.

"We're in this together, understand?" Kate asked us.

I nodded, resting my head against her shoulder. She smiled and then placed a kiss on the top of my head. "I'm so cold," Tina whispered a few minutes later.

I glanced up; her face was stained with tears, and her body seemed to tremble even more violently with each gust of wind that ripped through the shelter. "Don't worry; we're going to be fine," I whispered halfheartedly as the three of us shivered in misery.

I glanced up at Kate for support, but her strong determination seemed to have fizzled out as she sat there looking at the ground, seeming oblivious to Tina breaking down in front of her. "Do you remember when Mom use to take us to Hatfield farm?" Kate finally asked, probably breaking the silence in her best attempt to numb our pain with some idle conversation.

We both nodded, staring at her. "You two used to have so much fun up there picking the blueberries and apples. Mom and I would just sit back and watch you two for hours on end. You were both goofballs. I think Mom knew she wasn't going to live much longer, because she made me promise that I wouldn't let us be split apart," Kate explained.

Tina and I continued to stare at her in silence as Kate took a trembling breath and closed her eyes. I wanted to say something supportive, but I could only imagine the emotions that were flowing through her. "I promised her I wouldn't, but I need your guys' help as well. Okay? Promise me you won't do anything stupid, all right?"

I felt like her request was mostly directed to me as Kate opened her eyes and stared into mine. I gulped and gave her a nod. "I won't."

She smiled, I guess taking my word for it as she gave us each a kiss on the cheek. Soon afterward, Tina fell asleep, leaving Kate and I in silence. "Lance?" Kate asked me.

"Yes?"

Kate didn't say anything at first. She just stared at me for a moment and then, without warning, unclipped the long, gold pendant necklace around her neck and handed it to me. "You know what this is, right?" she asked.

I nodded as I unclipped the latch of the heart-shaped pendant. The tiny hinge swung open, revealing a picture of Tina, Kate, and me on the front steps of our old home in Dublin when Mom was still alive. "Kate, I can't ... Mom gave this to you."

I went to hand it back to her, but she pushed my offer away. "I want you to have it. Keep it with you always as a reminder of the love we have for you." She smiled, closing my hand with hers around the pendant.

"Thank you, Kate."

She huddled closer to Tina and me, giving another soft kiss on the cheek. "Good night, Lance," she whispered.

"Night, Kate," I whispered back.

Not long after that, we were serenaded to sleep by the merciless wind.

Early the next morning I felt the strong grip of a man giving me a light shake. I gingerly opened my eyes to discover that the man was Captain Murphy.

"Are you guys all right?" he asked.

"Yes, sir," I told him. He smiled as Tina and Kate gave him a nod as well.

"We have some breakfast ready over there if you guys are hungry," he offered.

I glanced over at a long line of women and children waiting for bread and then gave him a thankful nod. He smiled one last time, and then Captain Murphy and his men moved on to the next shelter.

"Are you two all right?" Kate asked.

Tina and I both nodded. She smiled, taking the blanket that we were huddled up in and folding it before we started our day. I walked over to the meal line where I was greeted by the soft, familiar voice of a female. "Hey, Lance."

I turned to spot the source of the greeting and realized that it was Rachel, the girl we had saved during the invasion.

"Hey, how'd you sleep?" I asked her as she moved aside in line, letting me hop in with her.

"Horrible. That wind was awful," she complained.

I muttered my agreement. "Did you find someone to sleep with?"

She shook her head. "I made my own shelter; a few of the rebels helped out."

"Cool. They seem like pretty good guys; I'm thankful they found us," I told her. I glanced at a pair of the rebels as they walked by, weapons slung over their shoulders, chatting to one another.

"I hear you're one of them," Rachel noted.

I glanced away, kind of embarrassed. She giggled, giving me a light bump with her hip as a smile spread across her face. She had a beautiful smile—the kind of smile that could keep you warm all night just thinking about it.

"Don't be embarrassed, Lance. I'm proud of you stepping up to defend our country from the fiends," she told me. An affectionate twinkle present in her eyes.

I couldn't help a smile from spreading across my face as I blushed in embarrassment. "Thank you, Rachel,"

She returned the smile, giving her long, blonde hair a swipe with her hand. She seemed to be thinking about something. "I'm going to join them to someday," she told me.

"Really?" I asked.

"What?" she responded, confused.

"Oh, it's nothing. It's just that ... well, I hope you don't get offended or anything, but you're a ... well, you're a girl," I told her, finally spitting it out.

She laughed. "Girls can fight too, Lance." I smiled as she mimed a playful punch to my chin, stopping as it hit.

"Where'd you grow up?" I asked her as we started to get close to the end of the line.

"East Dublin. I went to Saint Catherine's. What about you?" she asked.

"North Dublin."

"You went to George P. Vanier?" she asked.

I nodded, "How old are you?" she continued.

"Thirteen." I paused. "You?"

"Fourteen," she told me.

"Geesh, nearly old enough to be my grandmother," I joked. We both laughed. I was about to ask her about her family when we were interrupted by the rebels serving breakfast.

"Would you like some jam on that, bro?" one of the men asked me.

"No thank you. Butter's fine," I told him.

He handed me my two pieces of toast on a napkin. I smiled thankfully and waited for Rachel to get hers before following her off to the side where we found an abandoned log to sit on. "Mmm." I heard her mutter in satisfaction.

I glanced over to her and nodded in agreement as I ate my breakfast. "Don't think we're going to be saying that in a few weeks from now when this is all we're eating," I told her.

"A few weeks?" she asked.

I stared at her, confused by the statement.

"We probably only have enough bread for a few days," she told me, a serious tone taking over her voice.

I nodded in agreement, not having thought about that. "I'm sure they will send out scavenging parties soon for more food. Don't worry; Captain Murphy wouldn't let us go hungry," I told her, complete confidence behind my statement.

She laughed as she nodded in agreement. Once breakfast had finished, the rebels rounded up everyone and immediately began reconstruction. We spent the large majority of the day working on the frame of our meal hall.

"Yo, man, can you help me out?" someone called over to me as a few of the rebels and I searched deeper into the forest for logs, branches, and other materials required to build the meal hall.

The voice came from a dark-skinned teenager around my age. "Sure, man," I said, going over to him. We dug a log out of the ground with our hands and then hoisted it up onto our shoulders. The rough bark digging into our flesh made it a much more difficult job then one would have thought.

"Thanks a lot," he said as we set it down with all the other materials back at camp.

"No problem," I replied wiping some sweat from my forehead with my arm as I glanced around at everyone busily working.

I spotted Rachel off to the side weaving together thin branches of pine trees for the roof. The sound of the teenager talking jolted me back to the conversation. "My name's Grant," he told me, offering his hand.

"Oh. Lance," I said with a firm nod, grabbing his hand and giving it a shake. I tried to sneakily glance back to Rachel, but she spotted me just as I started tearing my eyes away from her.

"You got a thing for that girl?" he asked.

"No," I replied firmly.

"Then why are you blushing?"

"I'm not," I objected with a grin. We both laughed. "Maybe a little," I admitted

"She has eyes for you too, man."

"You think so?" I asked.

"For sure. She keeps glancing over to us. Why don't you go talk to her?" he suggested.

I glanced back at Rachel nervously, "I don't know," I muttered to him.

"Oh, come on. Grow a set," Grant told me with a laugh, egging me on.

He gave me a little push in her direction, forcing me to gather my thoughts as I walked over to Rachel, who was still preoccupied with the pine furs she was weaving. "Hey, do you need a hand with that?" I offered approaching her side.

She glanced up to me, a smile spreading across her face. "Sure. Thank you, Lance; that's so sweet."

I let an inward sigh of relief wash over me as I sat down beside her. Rachel passed me a pile of pine furs, and I began to weave them in silence at first until some idle conversation overcame us.

"So did you get split from your family or something?" I asked after we ran out of idle conversation to preoccupy ourselves with.

"Sort of," she began timidly. "I was walking home from my friend's house when the invasion started. Those metal meteorites the fiends came down in were like bombs." She paused as her voice began to quiver; I saw a stray tear fight its way down her beautiful face.

"I had seen it sailing through the air.... My mother was peering through the window of my home. I think she saw me, and then it struck. Nothing was left of the house." Rachel stopped talking as the tears finally overtook her.

"I'm sorry, Rachel.... I'm so, so sorry," I whispered, wrapping an arm around her as I tried my best to be comforting.

She thanked me and buried her head into my chest. I stroked her hair, and she began to settle down after a few more minutes passed by wiping away the remainder of the tears.

"What about you?" she asked as we resumed weaving the pine tree branches together.

"My father left my mother when she was pregnant with me and Tina, guess it was too much for him. Kate always told us that he was a quite man. He fought in the war of independence with this very rifle." I explained to her tossing a nod to the timber wolf slung on my back.

"Wow really?" Rachel asked glancing to the rifle.

I nodded continuing on with my story, "Mom was great—probably the most caring woman you would ever meet. She died of cancer three days before my thirteenth birthday," I ended, trying to shoo the emotions fluttering in my chest away by keeping my attention focused on weaving.

"I'm sorry to hear that, Lance," Rachel said.

I thanked her as silence briefly enveloped us. "Your sisters seem amazing," she told me.

"Yeah, Kate has always been there for us after Mom passed away. Tina can be a pest though," I told her with a smirk.

Rachel laughed, glancing up from her weaving. I returned the smile as our eyes locked for a split second. "Isn't that what sisters are for?" she asked playfully.

I shrugged with a laugh, tearing my eyes away from her beautiful smile. "If you want, you could sleep with us tonight," I offered, nodding over to Tina and Kate who were busily improving our shelter.

"Really?" she asked.

"Sure, why not? We have a blanket; it probably beats sleeping by yourself," I told her.

"Awesome; that sounds great. Thank you so much," she said, accepting my offer.

"Hey, Lance, this meal hall isn't going to build itself," Captain Murphy called out to me.

"I'm working on the roof, sir," I called back over to him, holding up a section of the roof I had weaved together.

"Get your lazy ass over here," the rebuttal came flying back. A smirk spread across his face as his attention shifted back to his men.

"Got to run," I muttered in embarrassment, quickly getting up to my feet.

Rachel giggled. "I guess so."

"Talk to you later?" I asked.

"For sure." She replied.

I gave her a wink and then jogged over to Captain Murphy's side. "Did you need something, sir?"

"Give me a hand with this log," he grunted.

We leaned it up against the frame. It was too tall, so we lowered it back down, marked off the proper length, and then sawed it off before laying it back down against the frame and nailing it in place. It was a good thing the rebels had stolen supplies from a local hardware store about twenty minutes from our camp, because without the tools, we would never have been able to build the camp.

"I seen you over there chatting with that girl," Captain Murphy began.

I felt myself blushing as I tried to convince him that Rachel was just a friend. "It's nothing to be embarrassed about, son," he noted. "You're going to treat her right though. Understand?"

"Of course sir." I promised.

He smiled and then gave me a pat on the back. "I know you will. I guess we can handle things around here you better get back to working on that roof," he said, a sly smile on his face.

I glanced back to Rachel giving him a thankful nod and then returned to her side, she smiled welcoming me back as the sun beat down on the two of us. She began talking again. I couldn't take my eyes off her.

All it took was that day for me to realize I had found something that many would never find in an entire lifetime, the one thing that everyone yearned for, true love.

# Chapter 3

CAPTAIN MURPHY CALLED A surprise meeting for all the rebels that night. I walked down an overgrown path accompanied by the dull rays of moonlight that made their way through the forest's canopy above. As the path came to an end, it revealed a hidden lake tucked away at the foot of the hill.

Members of the PLF where huddled around a small fire as the dull sounds of a radio played in the background. "What's going on?" I whispered to Grant.

"I don't know. Murphy says there is supposed to be a big announcement tonight," he replied.

"From who?"

Grant shrugged. I glanced around the group. Everyone remained silent staring at the radio, its shadow flickering in the fire. Five minutes passed before people started to get antsy.

"Maybe it's not going to happen tonight," someone suggested, followed by a wave of agreements.

"Shhh, have faith. It will happen," Captain Murphy whispered to us.

Everyone went quiet, plunging the group back into silence. Another five or ten minutes passed by before the radio made a weird coughing sound, then sprung to life with the voice of Canada's prime minister.

"Good evening, citizens of Canada. I would first like to send my deepest condolences to the families and friends of those who have sacrificed so much in the past few days due to this tragic event. I have gathered you all here tonight to hear my words. Take up arms against the invaders; don't let them take what is ours. Our country has a history of many battles being fought. We have not lost those, and we will not lose this one. I have signed a treaty with President Ovachekin of the United States of America, which opens our boarders and strengthens our bound as both countries battle this imminent threat to mankind hand in hand. This will be my final act as the prime minster of Canada, for I am hereby stepping down from my position. May you all fight with honor. Thank you, and God bless you." The recording paused for a moment and then began playing again in a continuous loop.

"Wow," someone muttered, taking the words from my mouth.

"So the fiends invaded America too?" someone else spoke up.

"Probably. How can we know for sure? For all we know, they could have invaded the entire world," someone else replied.

"All right, quite down, boys. So you've heard it from the man himself—we're in this thing for the long run. I want you all to get a good night's sleep, and tomorrow we will continue with the construction of the camp and start sending out patrols to guard the outer cordon," Captain Murphy ordered.

"Lance, stay here," He added as everyone was dismissed and began to disperse back up the hill to their shelters.

"Sir?" I asked. Taking a seat beside him, I could feel the beach's sand shift under my weight.

There were five other soldiers who had stayed behind and were sitting on the log opposite of myself and Captain Murphy. "Everyone, this is Lance," he said, introducing me to the others.

They nodded to me and then returned there stares back to the fire. "These men are some of the best I have," Captain Murphy told me. "They will teach you the tools of the trade and mold you into the fine soldier I know that you're capable of becoming,"

I nodded my thanks.

"Sir?" a timid voice called from behind us.

We all turned to see who it was; I could feel confusion spread across my face as I realized it was Rachel's thin body emerging from the shadows. Captain Murphy glanced from me back to her, clearly just as confused. "You should be sleeping with the others, Darling," he called over to her.

She stopped in front of us and then stared down at the ground, fidgeting ever so slightly. "I want to fight, sir. Let me join the resistance, please."

I glanced over at the others as they began to laugh. Captain Murphy shot them an angry look. I felt bad for Rachel as I saw her begin to blush in embarrassment, probably feeling foolish for asking to join a resistance that was composed mostly of grown men.

"Shut up," Captain Murphy barked angrily at his men.

They instantly went quiet. He motioned for them to leave, and they did, giving Rachel a few apologetic looks as they passed.

"I'm sorry about those guys, sweetie. They can be a little inconsiderate at times," Captain Murphy told her.

She gulped and then gave him an understanding nod. "So why should I let you join the People's Liberation Force?" he asked her gently.

"Well, um—" Rachel shifted around in place. "I want to kill the fiends," she said, although it wasn't very convincing.

"Why?" he asked her.

"Because they killed my family, sir," she replied more firmly.

He went silent; I could tell he was considering the possibility of allowing her to join. "Fighting with your emotions is a sure way to get yourself killed, dear. Do you think your mother would want her only daughter to die the same way as she did? Who would live on to pass your family's memories?" he asked.

She went silent, thinking for a moment. I knew there was no good answer to that question; Captain Murphy had a good point. A few tears began to trickle down her face as she looked at him. "Please," she begged, wiping away the tears while trying to stand up straight and confident.

"Can you do twenty-five push-ups?" he asked her.

She nodded. I knew that was a lie, and so did Captain Murphy. "Prove it," he told her.

Obediently she got down to the ground and started doing them. After about five or six, she was quivering, and her form began to turn sloppy.

"I don't want to see none of those girl push-ups either," Captain Murphy barked at her like a drill instructor.

I could hear her struggling for breath as she reached fifteen, collapsing into the dirt as her arms gave way.

27

"Are you quitting?" he asked her heartlessly.

I felt bad for her, but I knew he was seeing how much heart she had. "No," she said, panting for air as she began to get back up to her shaking knees.

"Then why aren't you showing me that you can do twenty-five push-ups?" he asked. "Wipe away those tears, young lady. You think the fiends are going to care whether or not you're crying as they're killing everyone around you?"

She sniffled, wiping them away.

"Why haven't you started?" he asked her.

"I'm tired," she mouthed back saucily.

He got up from the log beside me and kneeled down right in her face. "Don't you ever raise your voice to me," he yelled. "You understand?"

"Ye … ye … yes, sir," the quivering response came.

"You think this is a game?" he asked her.

"What if you and Lance went out on a patrol together, and he was shot? He would die, because you're too out of shape to drag him to safety," Captain Murphy yelled.

She resumed crying as she began to do more push-ups.

"Fifteen, sixteen seventeen," Captain Murphy counted. "Come on, Rachel. That one doesn't count; get all the way up there. Eighteen, nineteen, twenty, twenty-one. That one doesn't count either. I wanted twenty-five real push-ups." He put his hand under her belly right by the ground.

"If you don't hit my hand, it doesn't count." He barked at her much like a drill instructor would.

Rachel gasped for air, doing the final four push-ups successfully. I felt myself jump for joy inside a little bit as Captain Murphy's expression softened while he took on a fatherly role, helping her up to her feet. She was covered from head to toe in dirt, tears of joy in her eyes and snot running down her nose uncontrollably.

"Good job, Rachel," Captain Murphy congratulated her. "You have heart, and that is one thing you can't teach a soldier." He gave a pat on her back before wrapping his arm around her.

She stared up at him in shock before returning the hug.

"What do you think, Lance? Should we give her a shot?" Captain Murphy called over to me.

I saw her stare at me, a pleading look in her eyes. "If she wants to defend our people from the fiends, who are we to stop her?" I asked him with a shrug.

He smiled, nodding in agreement as he glanced back down to Rachel. "Welcome to the People's Liberation Force."

# CHAPTER 4

O NCE RACHEL JOINED THE resistance, everything seemed to fall into place for me around camp. The construction was progressing without a hitch. Rachel and I had started our training with the men in Alpha Squad, and it seemed like even though we had all been through so much, somehow everything was going to work itself out.

I couldn't tell you how long it was—maybe a few weeks or even a month went by of peace and quiet—and then one sunny summer morning we had our first encounter.

"*Halt!*" the cry from the camps guard came from a watchtower.

I whirled around and instinctively reached for my pistol; Rachel was right by my side as we jogged toward the source of the commotion. I stopped short of the guard tower when I spotted Brent, one of the guys I worked with in Alpha. He was in the middle of a path that headed west out of camp holding ten men at gunpoint. He was being backed up by the sentry in the wooden tower we had built a few days earlier.

One of the men took a step forward toward Brent, I guess as a way to distinguish himself as the leader of his small rebel group. I studied them. They looked like hardened veterans;

they had pistols strapped to their legs, bulletproof vests, and ballistic eyewear, along with an array of small arms ranging from mortars, rocket launchers, machine guns, snipers, and assault rifles with M203s.

"These guys are professionals. They didn't get caught by accident," I whispered to Rachel.

She nodded in agreement.

"What's going on here?" Captain Murphy's voice sounded.

I spotted him striding toward us. I could see him assessing the situation in his mind, hopefully coming to the same conclusion I had. "Lower your weapon, boys. We're all friends here," he called out as he came to a rest beside Brent, motioning for the man in the guard tower to lower his weapon as well.

He glanced over to Rachel and me, sending us a reassuring wink as his attention shifted back to the soldiers who had stumbled upon our base. Rachel and I holstered our pistols obediently, leaning against the wooden frame of the guard tower to see what would take place next. The men all lowered their weapons as well as a sign of good faith, and then Captain Murphy and the man who had distinguished himself as the leader met halfway up the path where they greeted each other and began to talk among themselves.

Whatever was discussed they must have agreed on, because at the end of the conversation, they were all smiles and shaking hands. "Come here, guys; it's all right," Captain Murphy called to us, motioning for the PLF to come great our new guests.

"This is Lieutenant Stark and his men from the 101st Airborne," Captain Murphy introduced us.

"American?" I asked. I was confused, as I had not heard of that unit before.

Brent gave me a nod before returning back to greeting the Americans. "Why don't you two show our guests to the transit hut? They must be tired from the long journey here," Captain Murphy suggested politely to Rachel and me.

We nodded and both smiled to the Americans, who followed us to a large hut we had just built a week or so earlier in the center of the camp as a way to get information. Our camp's interrogator would come to the hut and try to disseminate information from the group. He would then gather their names and ages so that there was proper documentation of who was living in the camp before they built their own shelters. Once we showed them the hut, they all went inside, thanking us as they dropped their kits in exhaustion and leaned against the wooden walls of the hut.

Rachel and I watched them for a few minutes just to make sure there wasn't any funny business, and then a few senior PLF members came in and relieved us from our post.

"Well, something like that doesn't happen every day, eh?" I asked Rachel as we walked back to the north guard tower we were working on.

"It sure doesn't," she said.

We busied ourselves for the rest of the morning building a fifteen-foot tall ladder to attach to the guard tower, finishing just in time for lunch. "What are you guys up to?" Grant greeted us as Rachel and I sat at our usual log to eat our warm bowls of soup.

"Nothing much," I muttered, glancing up from my bowl.

I noticed a girl tagging along by his side. She appeared to be about our age—probably fourteen or fifteen—and was tall with an athletic build and long brunet hair. I had seen her around camp with him a lot lately but hadn't ever had an actual conversation with her. I felt Rachel give me a hard shot to my ribs with her elbow, snapping me back to reality.

I returned my attention to my soup in embarrassment. "How are you, Ellie?" Rachel called over to the mystery girl. I figured it was her way of letting me know the girl's name.

"Not bad. The weather's nice; can't complain," Ellie called back over to Rachel with a light smile. She shooed away her long brunet hair as she blew on her soup to cool it down.

"So are you over in Charlie with Grant?" I asked her, confused.

Ellie nodded. "I just got transferred over there last week from Delta to do some training with them. What about yourselves? Are you guys still being trained?" she asked Rachel and me.

"Yeah, we're almost done, though. Brent and the rest of the boys think we're about ready for a combat patrol," I told her proudly.

"I did my first yesterday," Grant said, speaking up as he ate his soup. "It's just as boring as a normal patrol; only difference is you have, like, fifty extra pounds of kit." We all laughed.

"Hey, what are you kids doing?" Brent called over to us as he passed by.

"Nothing much. What are you saying?" I asked as he

came over to our group, resting his hands on his hips as he stopped to chat with us.

Brent was a pretty down to earth guy; he had been in the military under Captain Murphy's command before the invasion. He was in his early twenties and had kind of become a big brother for me and Rachel to look up to.

Whenever we didn't understand something during training, he was always there to give us a hand whereas most of the others just viewed Rachel and me as an extra burden that they had to take care of.

"So are you two ready for the hunting patrol this afternoon?" he asked us.

We both nodded, which he returned with a smile. "You got your ballistics, gloves, hunting kit, and all that other stuff, right?" he asked.

"Yep," we both replied.

"All right. Well, I'll see you two at thirteen hundred hours then."

"Over at the east gate?" I called to him as he began to walk away.

He glanced back with a nod, pointing in the direction where the guard tower was and where we had met the Americans that morning. "Just over there," he called before turning back around and joining a group of his buddies over by a fallen tree.

"He seems like a good guy," Grant said.

Rachel and I nodded. "What's your leadership like?" I asked him and Ellie.

"Shitty," Ellie responded.

The four of us cracked up laughing as we finished up our soup. We parted ways soon after, getting ready for the afternoon's events. I glanced over to the medical hut and spotted Tina and Kate. They watched in silence as Rachel and I threw on our gear.

"Are you ready to go?" I asked Rachel, trying to ignore the piercing stare Kate was giving me.

"Uh-huh," Rachel muttered, slipping on her gloves and then picking up her assault rifle.

"No good-bye?" Kate asked me moodily as Rachel and I passed by to leave.

"Sorry. I know this is hard on you. I just wanted to make it as painless as possible," I told her, giving Kate a hug good-bye and nodding to Tina.

"Hard on me?" she asked.

"You guys are just kids, Lance. They shouldn't be using you as soldiers," Kate said. "There are plenty of other fit men around here."

"Everyone has to contribute, Kate," I replied with a shrug.

She let out one of those annoyed sighs girls do when they don't get their way, which I ignored. I turned back around and quickly walked away with Rachel by my side.

"What's wrong with her?" Rachel asked once we were out of earshot.

"Nothing," I answered. "She's just worried that I'm going to be killed."

"Aren't you?" Rachel asked.

I shrugged. "When it's my time to go, it'll happen. Nothing we can do to stop it," I said.

Rachel laughed. "That's kind of a morbid way to think, isn't it?"

"Not really; its destiny," I explained to her with a wink.

She smiled, giving me a playful push with her elbow as

we came to a stop under the east guard tower. We both took a seat on the ground as we waited for the others. "So it was destiny that brought us together?" Rachel asked playfully.

I laughed. "I guess. Maybe a little bit of luck played into it as well," I suggested.

She smiled; it wasn't her usual friendly smile though. It was more of an affectionate, caring one. I returned it, our eyes meeting briefly, although it felt like an eternity.

I accidently dropped the cam paint I had in my hand, which fell innocently to the ground. "I got it," we both said simultaneously.

"Ouch," I grunted as our heads collided.

I rubbed it in pain as Rachel handed me my cam paint before bringing her hand up to her own head. We glanced at each other and then broke into laughter. "We're pathetic," she giggled.

We were both turning red with laughter, I nodded my agreement. Our moment was cut short as the usual playful insults came flying our way. "Oh great. We're taking the daycare out for a walk today," a strong, buff-looking guy named Luke said to his friend Chris as they arrived beside us.

"Maybe if you lay off the roids, Luke, you wouldn't be such an angry person," I suggested.

He laughed, I guess a little bit taken back by my boldness. "Feisty one this afternoon, eh?"

The four of us laughed. Five more minutes passed before Brent and Jessie arrived, completing the roster for our squad. The patrol was nothing out of the ordinary; our main objective was to bring a deer back to camp, but anything would do.

Luckily for us, it looked like the beautiful day was going

to hold up, which meant perfect hunting weather. Brent took point with Rachel and me behind him as he showed us a few tricks for hunting.

He raised his hand to signal a halt, motioning for Rachel and me to watch him as he pulled out a string and wire, turning it into a noose. "See?" he whispered as he set it up under a log where a small hole went through both sides.

"When the little bugger is running from a predator, he will pass through this hole; his neck will go through that wire, catch from his momentum, and then tightening until it's lights out for the little guy," Brent explained to us.

We nodded our thanks, and then he motioned for us to rejoin the ranks with the others as we got up and began walking deeper into the forest. After a few hours of walking probably three or four kilometers in a continuous circle around our camp's perimeter, Brent raised his hand, signaling another halt.

We did, silence enveloped the area once again. I heard a crack and then some rustling from a bush about fifty meters off to our left. To our joy, a full-grown buck emerged from the brush.

Unaware of our presence, it stopped in the middle of the small field and bent its head to chew on a clump of grass. I held my breath, praying to myself for Brent not to miss as I watched him raise his rifle and take aim. The shot rang out.

I saw the buck flinch as the bullet sailed right through its chest. It raised its head and looked over at us as if already knowing its fate, not even attempting escape. "Sorry, buddy," I heard Brent whisper to himself.

The buck took a few wobbly steps, its feet faltered and

it fell to the ground, succumbing to its wound. "Aw, poor guy," I heard Rachel squeak, a sad tone in her voice.

I placed my hand on her shoulder. To be honest, I felt the same way. As much as I knew we needed the deer to provide food to our camp, there was still that little part of me that wished Brent would have missed, allowing the deer to escape death unscathed.

"Well, kids, that's the circle of life; one must die for another to live," Luke called to Rachel and me as he pulled out his huge hunting knife. He stood up from his cover and walked over to the deer in order to gut it so we could take it to camp for meat.

"Why do you always have to be such an asshole?" Brent muttered to Luke as he walked by.

Luke turned to us as he broke the tree line into the opening where the deer was. "Guess it comes naturally," he called to us with a shrug.

There was a sharp crack of a rifle that rang out from the opposite end of the forest. I watched it tear right through Luke's chest; blood instantly began pouring from his mouth as he fell to the ground, clutching the wound.

"*Contact!*" Brent screamed.

The entire tree line in front of us exploded with the muzzle flashes of rifles and machine guns. We all dove for cover behind what little shelter was provided. I glanced at Chris, who began opening up on the tree line with his machine gun spraying wildly. Rachel was frozen in fear, cowering behind a rock.

I shouldered my timber wolf, taking a breath to steady my aim. The head of a fiend in human form poked up from behind a log, and I fired, connecting with my target and instantly killing him. "Come on, Rachel! Open up on them!" I tried to encourage her, pointing across the field in the direction for her to fire.

My words seemed to snap her back into reality as bullets hissed by us, dangerously close. She gulped, peeking around the rock to the source of the gunfire. She nodded to me and took aim through her rifle's scope, beginning to return fire on them.

"Help me! Please help me!" came the continues cries of sorrow from Luke as stray bullets from the crossfire bounced around his body, coming close to ending his life with each ricochet that passed.

"Stay down, Luke! Stay there; stop moving!" Brent kept shouting to him over the deafening sound of gunfire between the humans and the fiends.

I glanced at Jessie, our squad's signaler who was relaying information back to our camp through the radio. Three fully transformed fiends came crashing through the tree line in their beast form. They raced across the open field, trying to reach us but falling short by about twenty feet.

It took so many rounds to kill them that I hoped they wouldn't catch on and just do a blind rush on us. We held our ground for twenty minutes. By this time, Luke had fallen silent.

I was running dangerously low on ammunition sliding in my last magazine just as Charlie team showed up to reinforce our position as dusk began to set in around us.

"Holy shit!" I heard Grant yell as he took cover beside me, staring at the barrage of tracers racing back and forth between us and the fiends.

Brent peeled back, rendezvousing with the leader of Charlie and filling him in on the situation. "We need to start laying mortars on them," someone suggested.

"No, we can't. Luke is still out there," came Brent's rebuttal.

"Is he even still alive?" another guy from Charlie asked.

There was silence for a moment between them. The only sound was the continuous cracking of gunfire. "We don't even know if he's still alive, Brent. We need to get mortars down range, or we're all going to be in a grave with him," a third man shouted.

I glanced back at Brent. He bit his lip as he made what must have been the hardest decision of his life. "Call them in," he finally said.

I glanced out at the field; I could still see the silhouette of Luke's body lying there in the grass. "Cover me, Grant," I whispered, taking off all my gear.

"Huh? What? No, Lance, come back here!" Grant yelled at me as he tried to grab for my leg.

It was too late, I crawled away, staying as close to the ground as humanly possible while rounds hissed by inches overhead. "Get back here, Lance!" I heard the angry cry from Brent chase after me.

I was already halfway there. Ignoring Brent's angry calls, I crawled farther and farther into the field where I came to a rest by Luke's side. "Luke?" I whispered, nervously giving him a shake as I feared the worst.

"Lance?" the weak gurgle of a response came back.

I sighed in relief, grabbing hold his vest's collar. "I got you, buddy. Just hold on," I told him. As I dragged the both of us along the ground, he screamed in pain.

It was no easy feat to drag the grown man across the ground. I reached out to find something to place my hand on and then pull us both forward, grunting in exertion.

Sweat poured down my face; the smell of carbon and sounds of war all around chilled my blood, making me want to curl up in a ball and play dead, but I couldn't let Luke die. I reached out; grasping my hand around a rock then pulled us farther forward.

I felt the rough grab of Brent and Grant as they dragged me to safety once I had reached the tree line. "Quick! I need a medic over here!" Brent yelled, pushing me aside and ripping off Luke's gear to inspect his wound.

Two medics appeared by our sides, getting him onto the stretcher and whisking him away to the safety of the camp. "You did it! You're one crazy son of a bitch," Brent yelled at the top of his lungs. I could barely make out the smile across his face that went from ear to ear through the thickness of the dark night.

"Lance, Lance, Lance, oh thank God!" Rachel cried, coming to my side and taking a knee as she set down the gear that I had left behind to save Luke.

She wrapped her arms around me. "Don't you ever do that again!" she scolded.

I tried to say I was sorry, but before I could finish the sentence, she tilted her head and kissed me. We stared at each other for a moment, oblivious to the sound of war around us. She smiled; I guess not knowing what to say. I was also at a loss for words.

She leaned forward and gave me one last kiss and then, without even a good-bye, scampered back off to her firing position, spraying a few shots on her way. I shook my head kind of confused and wondering if I had just imagined what had happened when the hiss of a round nearly missing me snapped me back. I regained my senses as I hit the ground, throwing my gear back on and grabbing my timber wolf. I then crawled back to my position where Grant was firing from.

"You got some set of balls on you!" Grant called to me as we began firing at a fiend machine gunner off to the right of the field behind a rock.

"I don't know about that. I'm pretty sure I pissed myself," I called back to him.

He laughed. "Take cover! Friendly mortars inbound!" The message came racing across the line.

A para flare shot up into the air, lighting up the area as we ducked. It was quickly followed by the mortars smashing into the ground about a hundred meters away, shaking the ground like an earthquake. Grant and I both looked at each other in fright. He was about to say something when I saw him pause and squint to get a better look at me.

"What?" I asked, confused.

"Is that lipstick on your cheek?" he yelled in disbelief over the pounding of the mortars. I laughed with a nod, giving him a wink. "Aw, man, come on. How come a brother never gets any love out here?" he yelled with a smirk as he gave me a hard punch to the shoulder.

"It's the looks, man. That's all I can say—it's the looks," I shouted back as we both broke into laughter, taking cover as the mortars' reign of terror ended followed by the fiends deciding to retaliate with an unforeseen amount of machine-gunfire.

The battle raged on for the entire night, forcing every soldier who was left in the camp to come and fight it out with the fiends, but we held our ground. I heard that three PLF soldiers had been killed and five wounded, but that was just a rumor floating around the line. As the morning began to peek through the tree line, we were becoming pretty complacent with the battle, smoking and joking while occasionally returning fire as we reached a stalemate, both sides having to conserve ammunition.

"I think they've retreated," I muttered about two hours later, having not seen anyone in nearly an hour.

"What's that?" Brent asked, coming over to the fortified little bunker Grant and I had constructed.

"They're not there anymore," I repeated to him.

"Are you sure?" he asked, peering across the mist-covered field to the quiet woodland ahead.

"One hundred percent," I muttered, still staring through my scope.

Brent took a puff of his cigarette as the three of us stared across for any signs of life. "Do you guys smoke?" he asked.

"We do now," Grant said to him.

Brent laughed, taking one last puff and then giving the rest of it to Grant and me to share. "Attaboy, get 'er into you. I'm going to go talk to higher-ups and see what they want to do," Brent said.

I could hear the pride in his voice as he handed me the cigarette with a wink before leaving our post. I'm pretty sure it was a moment in my life that I would never forget as I returned my attention to the open field and took a long drag of the cigarette then handing it off for Grant to finish. I took a quick glance back, spotting Brent, Captain Murphy, Lieutenant Stark, and a few others all huddled in a group discussing something amongst themselves.

Murphy had seen me staring at him. I instantly tore my eyes away, feeling embarrassed as I stared back out at the field. "You look like you need a break, Grant," Captain

Murphy called over to us once he had finished up his meeting with the others.

"Oh, I'm fine, sir," Grant called back as Captain Murphy approached our side.

"No, I insist. You've been working hard all night. Go back to camp and get some food and water into you; bring Ellie and Rachel with you as well," he added.

"Um, huh? Do you want us to come back once we finished?" Grant sputtered, probably not believing his ears.

Captain Murphy shook his head, lying down in Grant's old position. "Get some rest. We've got things under control around here now, son," he ordered Grant.

"Um ... Yes, sir?" Grant said, unsure of what to do.

I watched him stumble off down the line in search of Ellie and Rachel. I remained silent as we both stared out watching our arcs. I saw the Americans, led by Lieutenant Stark, kitting up. "I feel pretty honored right now," Captain Murphy told me.

Confused, I glanced over at him. "Sir?" I asked.

"It's not every day that I get to lie next to a hero," he explained.

I felt myself blushing as I remained silent. "You heard?" I asked.

He nodded. "I'm sure everyone has heard by now, Lance. It's very rare that I come across someone like yourself. It isn't in the human nature to be willing to sacrifice your own life for someone else, yet you did it so willingly."

"I ... ugh ... I'm not a hero, sir. I wasn't even thinking; I just did it."

He laughed, giving me a pat on my back. "You saved

Luke's life, Lance. You will be rewarded for your bravery—I promise."

I remained silent, not knowing what to say as my attention shifted to the Americans who spaced out and began racing across the field, grenades at the ready. When they were about twenty meters away, they tossed the grenades into the tree line and dove to the ground. It shook in the order that they were thrown, accompanied by the loud explosions. I watched as they got back up and raced up over the dirt mound into the tree line, spraying wildly.

I didn't hear any return fire, and then a few seconds later, Lieutenant Stark came out of the woods, giving us the thumbs up. Captain Murphy returned it, glancing over to me with a smile. "Just like clockwork," he said and then motioned for everyone to get up.

"Alpha, come consolidate past the objective; everyone else, return back to base," Captain Murphy ordered.

Everyone obediently got up and shook out their legs while meeting with their buddies and discussing their individual war stories from the battle. Jessie, Brent, Chris, and I, as well as a medic named Richard, all followed Captain Murphy across the field. We passed the obliterated deer and the three dead bodies of the fiends we had killed when they tried to charge us.

Once we reached the other side, it was clear that we had won the fight. There were no signs of dead fiends, but a lot of the ground was covered in their purplish blood and shell casings. "How many would you say we got?" I asked Brent.

He shrugged. "Looks like ten or twenty," he said with a light smirk.

"They certainly did leave in a hurry," Chris muttered,

nodding toward a whole pile of live, nonfired ammunition that they'd left behind.

"I just wanted you boys to see what we've accomplished here," Captain Murphy explained to us as he approached my side and placed his hand on my shoulder. "Now let's gather up all the ammo we can and head back to camp. The fiends could have this place zeroed with artillery fire, so we don't want to hang around too long."

We all muttered our agreement as we gathered up what we could before making a quick exit back to camp. As we entered the perimeter of the camp, to no surprise Tina and Kate were the first there to greet me. "Lance!" an ecstatic Tina shouted at the top of her lungs.

"Hey, guys, what's up?" I replied.

"Don't 'Hey, guys, what's up?' me, mister.... Come here." Kate giggled, beckoning me toward her.

I did obediently, and then the three of us shared a hug. "We could hear the fighting from the medical hut," Tina explained.

I nodded. "It was pretty bad."

Kate and Tina both stared at me as if they didn't know what to say. "Well, we're just glad that you made it back to us," Kate spoke up.

"Aw, thanks, Sis," I grunted with a roll of my eyes.

The three of us laughed. "Well, we better let you get on your way. I'm sure you have other people you need to attend to," Kate added.

"Like Rachel!" Tina chimed in obnoxiously.

I swung a fist for her, but she was too quick nimbly avoiding it. "Shut up, you little brat." I grunted.

The three of us shared one last laugh and said our good-byes before parting ways. All the soldiers involved in the battle were treated like kings that night. Someone had killed a moose, so we were all feasting, singing, laughing, and drinking amongst ourselves.

An hour later, I found what I was really looking for. "Lance!" Rachel called excitedly waving to me as I spotted her at the outdoor bar.

She handed me a beer already looking pretty drunk herself by the goofy grin smeared across her face. I took a seat beside her and glanced around the outdoor bar. It wasn't much, but considering what we had for supplies, it was pretty decent.

The barstools and counter were made out of wood, while tree branches filled with leaves overlapping each other above served as a roof. "Whoops, sorry." Rachel giggled as her drink slipped from her hand.

"It's fine," I assured her.

I laughed as I called the bartender to serve her another drink. You could tell she hadn't drank before by her drunken behavior. I sipped on the beer she had given me in silence with her; she sat on my lap, cuddling with me as we listened to a few people reliving the events of the battle earlier in the day.

I found it funny how they were talking as if they had actually fought the entire battle when half of them hadn't even fired their guns. They weren't there to see an entire wall of machine guns open up on them or to watch Luke take that shot in the chest or even to watch that deer die just to be wasted needlessly. To forget the three lives that had been sacrificed and those who were lying up in the hospital probably fighting for their lives was such an insult.

I could feel myself getting annoyed by their stories as I drank. I hugged Rachel close while trying my best to tune them out as the others laughed drunkenly by the stories. "Can we go?" I whispered to Rachel.

"Huh? Why what's the matter?"

"Nothing. I just want to find somewhere a little quieter," I told her.

I could see in her eyes that she wanted to stay and drink, but I must have meant more to her. She gave me a lighthearted smile and a nod before following me away from the bar to one of the campfires where we both sat in silence watching the dull flicker of the flame illuminate the night sky around us.

Rachel giggled, glancing up at me. "What?" I asked, confused.

"You're so cute," she whispered.

I felt myself blushing. "Nuh-uh, you are."

She reached up, pulling my head down and giving me a kiss. I cleared my throat nervously and glanced around to see if anyone else was around. Rachel giggled again; she must have spotted my unease.

"It's okay, Lance. Don't be embarrassed. I get it; you're not ready. We can take our time," she whispered.

I gave her a thankful nod. She smiled, which I returned, placing a gentle kiss on her cheek. I felt her head rest into my chest; I hugged her close, our attention shifting back to the fire. A few hours passed by as we just sat in silence, comforted by one another's warmth.

"There's the man of the hour," Captain Murphy called out, finding us just as we were getting ready to get up and go to bed.

"Evening, sir," I replied as he sat down beside the fire with a devilish smile across his face.

"What?" I asked him.

"Remember how I said I'd repay you for saving Luke's life?" he asked.

"Oh, yes, sir. Don't worry about that, though; I don't want anything," I muttered, being a hundred percent sincere.

"I know you don't, but I did anyway, so enjoy your new shelter," he told me, nodding up behind us.

"Huh?" I asked, glancing behind me at the cave that was used for the headquarters building.

"It's yours," he congratulated me.

He held his hand up before I could protest and clinked his beer against mine, chugging it down before telling us good night and disappearing back into the crowd of celebrating soldiers.

"Wow," Rachel muttered staring down at me, a drunk smile of joy across her face.

"Yeah," I replied in disbelief.

"Want to go check it out?" she asked me, her voice littered with hopefulness.

I smiled as I glanced back up to the cave, deciding to make the best of it; after all, I did earn it in Captain Murphy's eyes. "Yeah, sure. Let's do it."

It was late by the time we got around to checking out my new home. I was pretty buzzed; Rachel, on the other hand, was completely wasted. "Oh geesh, watch yourself," I warned her as we stumbled up the rocky path toward the foot of the cave.

She giggled, not paying any attention to my warning as she grabbed my hand affectionately while we battled our way up the final row of rocks, coming to a rest at the foot of the cave. "This is huge!" she squeaked as she looked around the massive den.

I stood there speechless; Rachel had taken the words right out of my mouth. It was clear that Captain Murphy and his men tried to doll it up for us before we arrived. The floor had been swept; there were two military sleeping bags, air mattresses, and a platter of finger foods with wine and two slices of moose meat in the middle of the two sleeping bags.

Rachel practically dragged me over to the sleeping bags, popping open the bottle of wine and pouring us both a glass as we dug into the platter of food. "Mmm, this is amazing," I said while eating off the platter. The smoky, rich taste of the moose meat seemed to spring my taste buds back to life.

"No, you're amazing," Rachel whispered, a drunken smile on her face.

I felt myself blushing, unable to return the compliment. She spotted my embarrassment and began giggling as she finished her wine. Setting down the glass, she cuddled up to me as we lay down on the air mattresses. I stroked her gently and was rewarded a few minutes later by the light sounds of her snoring.

The next morning brought with it Morse code training. We were shaken awake by Brent; Rachel was still draped across me. "Looks like you kids had a fun night," he joked.

Rachel and I glanced at each other before cracking up with laughter. Brent left us to get ready for work. "Ugh, my head is pounding," Rachel muttered as we sat up and got ready to go.

"You're telling me," I grunted in agreement. "Where did I put those boots?"

"They're right here, silly." Rachel giggled, tossing the pair over to me.

"Thanks," I muttered, wishing my pounding headache would vanish. I put on the boots, tucking the pant legs in.

"Have you drank before?" Rachel asked as we got up, deciding to leave our weapons and gear in the cave.

"No, and I probably won't ever again," I muttered, shielding my eyes from the sun as we emerged from the entrance of the cave.

She giggled, hugging me close while we made our way down the steep path to the camp below. I could feel eyes on us as people spotted us coming from the cave. I'd never had a girlfriend before, and to be honest, I figured this of all places would be the last that I would find one.

However, Rachel played the part without a hitch. She kept me talking, I guess in her best attempt to eliminate the embarrassment. Once we reached our squad's training hut, we were greeted by the familiar faces of everyone.

Even Luke was there relaxing in a chair, his chest wrapped tight with bandages. "Hey, little man, thanks a lot for what you did out there. I owe you one," he told me as I walked by.

I stopped, glancing down as he offered me his fist to bump; I did politely with a faint smile. "Anytime, Luke."

Rachel and I then took our seats across from each other at a wooden bench in the back of the small hut. It felt so weird being with the squad now; it was as if we were a family. There was no more taunting each other or silly fights over nothing.

Everyone was just joking around, playing cards, and stuff like that. I don't think I'd ever seen morale so high. "All right, all right, quiet down, you lot, so I can ramrod through this lesson," Brent called to all of us as he came in taking out a stack of papers and then handing out a piece of paper and a pen to everyone.

"Morse code is one of the most primitive techniques used by modern-day militaries, but it is still, to this date, used and can be an effective means of communications if used properly. Captain Murphy has ordered me to teach you misfits this tool of the trade for the unlikely event that you are ever captured, in which case this will probably be your only lifeline—so listen up," he began.

I felt my hands go clammy as nerves set in. I was a slow learner when it came to reading and writing, so this was not going to be my favorite lesson at all. He took out a rock and began tapping it on the desk while telling us what letter each set of taps represented.

He proceeded to do that for the rest of the morning, teaching us the rest of the alphabet before we broke for lunch. When we came back, it was our practical. "All right, everyone, grab a partner and start practicing," he called from the front of the room, thereby ending his lecture.

I turned to Rachel who shot me a smile. "Ladies first," she teased.

I laughed, picked up my rock, and began to tap slowly on the desk for her to write down the individual letters which would form my message. "This as born?" Rachel muttered a moment later, looking down at her sheet confused.

"What?" I asked with a laugh, all I could do was shake my head.

"This is boring," I corrected her, "How does 'This as born' make any sense?" I asked with a laugh.

"I have no clue," she admitted with an embarrassed shrug. "I could have sworn that's what you were trying to say to mess me up."

I smiled. "You're silly. It's your turn," I said, picking up my pencil to write down her message.

I had been nervous, not wanting Rachel to find out that I had problems with reading and writing. After her performance though, there was no way I could do worse which kind of lifted an invisible weight off my chest.

She thought about her sentence for a second before beginning. I figured from the smile she had on her face that it was going to be something funny. I began writing down the letters she was taping on the desk trying my best to keep up.

When she was done, I looked down to see what I had spelled out: I-L-O-V-E-Y-O-U. I stared at it for a second, a little taken aback. I guess I shouldn't have been as surprised by her bold statement as I was.

I had been feeling the exact same way, the feelings growing stronger and stronger as each day passed. She gave me an anxious smile as I glanced up from the paper and caught her eyes. "What's it say?" she asked, playing dumb.

"I lone you?" I asked, glancing back down at the piece of paper putting on a mock confused look.

"Huh, no," she muttered, her smile fading as she thought I messed up the message.

She snatched the piece of paper from my hand and looked down at the message, which clearly read "I love you." She then looked up from it and back to me with a smirk. "You little shit. You had me going there for a second." She giggled.

I laughed, giving her a playful wink. "I love you too," I whispered back, placing my hand on hers affectionately.

She giggled, glancing over to the others. "They're looking, Lance," she warned me.

"Good," I whispered.

A smile spread across her face. I closed my eyes, meeting her halfway for the kiss, knowing things between us would never be the same.

# CHAPTER 5

*Three Years Later*

"Yo, Lance, it's our shift," Grant called to me.
"Give me a second," I said, glancing down to my lap where Rachel was snoozing.

I tried to gently lift her up and place her on the ground, but she woke up. "You have sentry duties?" she asked, wiping the sleep from her eyes.

"Yeah, I'll be back in an hour," I told her as I took off my hoodie and rolled it up in a pillow for her to sleep on.

"Make sure to bundle up, love. It's chilly out there," she warned with a sleepy yawn as she snuggled up in her sleeping bag.

"I will. Sweet dreams, babe," I said, kissing her good-bye.

I shouldered my timber wolf, throwing my hunter's tunic on, and then walked down from the entrance of the cave to where Grant was waiting impatiently. "Man, I hate being your fire team partner. I swear. We always start ten minutes late, because you got to tuck your girl in and say good-bye as if you were going away for a month's deployment," he complained as we walked the perimeter of the newly built huts below the cave.

A lot had changed in three years. We had managed to scavenge barbed wire fence for our perimeter, not to mention that our camp had expanded by a good fifty percent from its original size. We now even had a concrete bunker for the civilians to take shelter from artillery, and guard towers had been erected all along our perimeters.

"Don't be mad at me because you can't get any love from Ellie anymore," I shot back with a friendly shove.

"Are you kidding me? She digs big, strong resistance fighters such as me. It's just that four years happens to dampen the fire in a couple's relationship," he told me as he flexed his muscles.

"Yeah, tell me about it. Rachel's been so moody lately," I muttered.

He laughed, giving me a pat on the back. "Rocky weather on Love Island?" Grant asked playfully as we climbed up the north guard tower to relieve the two sentries.

"I guess. I don't know what's up with her half the time anymore," I muttered.

"It's simple. I happen to know all about women—she wants you to take it to the next level," Grant explained to me, a sly smirk on his face.

I rolled my eyes. "Yeah, well she's going to have to wait for the war to be over before that happens," I told him with a laugh.

He laughed in agreement. "Ellie's been acting the same way, man. Every time I take a knee to tie my shoes, I see her eyes light up before they instantly fill with disappointment."

We both broke into laughter until it hurt. "Women, eh?

Can't live with 'em; can't live without 'em," Grant noted. I nodded in agreement.

Our conversation was cut short by a rustle in the bushes below. "Do you hear that?" I asked.

"Yeah. Grab the spotlight," Grant whispered.

I grabbed the light, pointed it toward the source of the sound, and then flicked the bright beam of light on. Our buddy Tim stepped out of the bush in a daze, buckling his pants up as he shielded his eyes from the blinding light. "What the heck are you doing out of your barracks, Tim?" I called down to him.

"I had to go for a piss, asshole. Turn that shit off," came the annoyed reply.

I did obediently, leaning back over the ledge of the guard tower to interrogate him. "Why didn't you just go to the outhouses?" I asked.

"I wanted to go here. Sue me," he called back up angrily and then started heading back to the camp.

I felt my blood pressure rising, wishing I could just pop a round into his cocky ass. "Man, just let him go," Grant muttered, placing his hand on my shoulder.

"Everyone's such a hotshot around here. Kill a fiend, and suddenly you're the most badass soldier on the planet," I muttered in anger.

"They haven't been around as long as us. They'll grow up eventually and see that this shit is for real and not a video game," Grant replied as he lit up a smoke and took a puff before offering me one.

I waved his offer away, leaning against the wooden frame of the tower moodily as I listened for anymore intruders. "I wish Luke, Chris, and the other boys were still alive.

They'd put these new recruits in their place real fast," I muttered.

Grant nodded in agreement, finishing off his smoke and tossing it over the side. "I heard Brent is coming back from Golf Company soon."

"Really?" I asked in surprise.

He nodded. "I guess he missed good old India Company, eh?" Grant muttered with a smirk.

I returned the smirk, my spirits being raised by the good news of possibly seeing one of my old friends again. An hour passed by before two guys I didn't know climbed up the ladder to relieve us. We smiled, offered them a smoke, which they declined, and then climbed down the tower and headed toward our individual shelters.

"Want to meet up at the range tomorrow?" Grant asked as we got ready to part ways.

"Sure," I replied. We performed our secret shake, laughing as we split paths toward our shelter.

When I arrived back to the cave, Rachel was awake and combing her hair in the reflection of a puddle. "You look nice," I told her as I sat down, setting my weapons along the side of the rocky wall.

"Really?" she asked, lying down beside me and wrapping her arm around my waist.

"Uh-huh, I'm going over to the firing range tomorrow with Grant, would you like to come?" I asked her.

"Of course." she replied.

She smiled, readjusted herself under the blankets, and then patted her belly, inviting me to lay my head on her stomach. I did, letting sleep overcome me as she gently stroked my hair.

Rachel and I met Grant and Ellie down at the firing

range the next day. It was a mixture of work and fun. I tried to have loose training sessions like this one all the time.

"Nice shot," Rachel said, peering through her binoculars at the barely visible target off in the distance.

"Seven hundred-meter head shot," she informed me, setting the binoculars down with a smile.

I shot again. "One kilometer," she exclaimed.

I gave her my rifle to watch her practice. She was shooting nice until around five hundred meters, when she started missing most of her shots. "I guess that's why you're the sniper and I'm the spotter," she said, tapping her submachine gun.

I laughed in agreement, glancing over at Grant who was lying on the ground beside me and firing his machine gun in bursts. Grant, Ellie, Rachel, and I were all on the same squad now. I had risen my way up the ranks and been promoted to squad leader, so Captain Murphy decided to put me in charge of Foxtrot for our company.

The perk to being put in charge of a newly formed squad was getting your pick of the litter, so naturally I picked my three best friends without a second thought. "Man, I'm the backbone of this squad. I don't even know why I keep you guys around," Grant called to us as he stood up to inspect his mauled target.

"My looks, right?" I asked, pushing Rachel aside.

"Nuh-uh, it's mine," Ellie replied sarcastically while packing up her explosives.

"So you want to go catch a game of hoops this afternoon or what?" Grant asked once we had reached our daily allowance of ammunition.

"Yeah, for sure," I began to say.

"No, Lance is busy," Rachel interrupted.

I glanced over at Rachel, sending her a confused frown. Grant and Ellie stared at each other with a smirk. "All right. Well, when mom's done with you, come out and play with the big boys," Grant teased me, grabbing Ellie's hand before heading back to camp.

"Why did you do that?" I asked Rachel, shouldering my rifle.

"You've been ditching me for Grant this entire week. How do you think that makes me feel?" she asked as we walked along a path to the lake.

"He's my friend," I interjected.

"Well, I'm your girlfriend!" she shot back, looking to pick a fight with me.

"I figured you would want to chill with your friends this afternoon," I lied.

"Bullshit. You're so inconsiderate it's not even funny," she accused me, raising her voice and giving me a rough shove.

I knew she was working herself up into a fit, so I walked away. She, of course, chased after me. Ignoring her angry yells I put all my gear in our cave and changed into my gym gear.

"Don't ignore me, Lance!" she yelled. "You're not going down there!"

"Watch me," I muttered.

She swung her fist at me, but I dodged it, grasping onto her in a hug to prevent her from throwing another punch at me. "Stop it, Rachel!" I yelled back.

She stopped struggling and stared up at me; tears began running down her cheek as her lips thinned, quivering uncontrollably. I pushed her away.

"No, Lance, wait. Please, I'm sorry." She sniffled and

came back toward me with a hug as a peace offering, but I kept my hand out, not accepting her offer.

"I'm leaving, Rachel."

Her begs for me to stay were ignored as I turned on my heels and jogged down to the basketball court. We had plans to add cement to it someday, but for now the packed dirt regulation-sized area would do.

"I get Lance," Grant yelled, spotting me on the sideline.

We played a two-on-two against a ginger-haired kid named Junkin and his older brother Ryan, winning ten baskets to four with me scoring six of them. They paid us fifty dollars each, which was the standard amount for a win. You would think that with the fall of civilization money would no longer be used as currency, but Captain Murphy was big on economics.

He believed that one day, if we lived to see the end of the war, we would come out in the upper class, because a lot of civilians would have used their savings for food, water, and stuff like that. Sure, the money was useless for now, but one day when the war was over—well, if it ever was over—I planned on finding a nice little house down on waterfront property to buy and live in with Rachel for the rest of our lives. I saw her storm past the court out of the corner of my eye.

She glanced over to me and then quickly looked away, sitting with Ellie on the wooden bleachers off to the side. Grant and I were on fire; we had won five games in a row making two hundred fifty dollars each by the end of the night.

"Anyone else want a piece of this?" Grant offered the crowd with a cocky gesture of his hands.

No one stepped up, so we sat on the sideline and paid a little kid to go get us some water. "What's up with you and Rachel?" Grant asked as we wiped the sweat off, exhausted from our games. "I know for a fact she didn't let you come play."

"It's nothing," I replied, retrieving a glass of water from the kid who had returned.

"Come on, man. I saw her walk by. She was practically foaming at the mouth. Something's up," he insisted.

"We just had a stupid fight over nothing. That's all," I replied.

"It's your fault then," he told me.

"What? No, I just wanted to play ball," I protested.

"I know it's not your fault, dummy," he replied with a laugh, "but believe me, it's your fault. Get my drift? Just tell her that, and everything will be fixed. I promise."

"But that would mean it's always going to be my fault," I said, confused.

Grant let out a laugh and nodded in agreement. "That doesn't seem fair," I muttered.

"Life isn't fair," he responded, still laughing.

We sat there and watched a game on the other end of the court in silence. Halfway through I spotted Rachel and Ellie leaving, but my attention was shifted away as Grant went into one of his usual rants. "Man, if we resigned from the PLF, we could make like seven hundred a day just off of basketball," he told me.

I remained silent. I'd never quit the resistance. It had practically raised me into the man I had become.

"We got a mission for tonight," I told him, taking a piece of paper out from my pants pocket and handing it to him.

"A supply mission?" he asked, opening it up to read.

I nodded. "In and out. The fiends won't even know we were there."

"Make sure to have your silencers attached when we meet up at the rock tonight. Pass it on to Ellie as well when you see her," I told him as we got up to leave.

"All right. Peace, man," He called to me before walking down the sideline and disappearing behind a couple huts toward his shelter.

I dribbled the ball out to half-court and shot at the net a few times, not in any hurry to go back and deal with Rachel. To my surprise, after awhile, Ellie came out to the court. I passed her the ball, which she shot.

It sailed through the air into the hoop. "Rachel and I watched you and Grant playing today. You had some pretty sick moves out there," she said, breaking the silence.

"Thanks," I replied retrieving the ball and then passing it back out to her. "I'm going to assume you're not here to talk about basketball, though."

She smiled, motioning to the bleachers. We walked over together and sat down. "Word on the street is you and Rachel had a fight," she told me.

"Yeah, something like that I guess."

"She asked me to tell you she was sorry for spazzing out on you like that at the range," Ellie said.

"Why couldn't she tell me that?" I replied stubbornly.

"Oh come on, Lance. You know how girls are," Ellie replied, rolling her eyes.

We both laughed. "I don't know if Grant told you yet or not, but we have a mission for tonight," I informed her.

"Right on. What is it?" she asked.

"A supply mission—Grant has the details,"

"Well, I'd better get going then. Rachel wants you to go

to the lake when you're done playing basketball," Ellie told me as she got up to leave.

"Thanks for the talk, Ellie." I couldn't help sending her a smile

She smiled, giving me a nod, and then left. I rolled the basketball to a group of kids before walking down the path to the camp's lake. "Hey, babe, we got a mission tonight," I told Rachel, accidently spooking her as I came up behind her.

She turned to look at me as I sat down awkwardly beside her, passing a piece of paper with the mission details on it. "In and out?" she asked.

I nodded; she offered me her fist, which I tapped with mine. "So you're not mad?" she asked, staring at the setting sun in the distance.

"Nah, it was my fault. I was being selfish," I replied.

"You're a bad liar. Who told you to say that? Ha-ha, don't tell me. It was Grant, wasn't it?" she asked with a laugh. I laughed as well, knowing the jig was up.

"I'm sorry too—for putting you down in front of our friends," she said sincerely. "I woke up in a bad mood and just couldn't get rid of it all day."

"It's cool. Let's just put it behind us," I suggested, getting up and wiping the dirt off my clothes.

"All right," she replied, holding her hand up to me hopefully. I grabbed it and helped her up. She held my hand as we walked up the path, past the huts, to our cave. Once we got there, I sat down and took apart my sniper rifle in order to clean it before that night's mission. Rachel did the same to her MP5 and handgun.

Once I was satisfied with my weapon, I attached its

silencer and did the same to my handgun. "I hate silencers," I told Rachel as she started to camouflage her face.

"Why?" she asked.

"They throw off the accuracy and power of the shot," I replied beginning to cam up my own face as well.

"True, but at least the whole place doesn't know you're there," she replied.

I attached my headset and put on my uniform boots and gloves, along with the backpack full of ammunition. "Hey, Grant, you there?" I asked into the headset, shouldering my sniper rifle and getting up.

"Yeah, where are you?" he answered.

"We're heading to the north rock. Meet us there," I called back into the microphone.

"Roger," came the reply.

Grant and Ellie were already waiting for us at the rock when we arrived. "Hey, what's up?" we all greeted each other, trying to lighten the mood with a few jokes before we set off on our mission.

"All right, let's do this—lights off; night-vision goggles on," I ordered.

They did so obediently, and then we began to trudge through the dense foliage of the Harush Forest toward Dublin. You would think with night-vision goggles that would be an easy task, but believe me, it is one of the most difficult things you will ever do in your life. Night-vision goggles are great, but when you wear them, you feel like you have zero depth perception, which makes for a lot of stumbling and tripping as you navigate your way through the forest.

We became silent as the silhouettes of tall bombed-out buildings began to appear in the distance. "Grant and Ellie, you're getting sidearms and ammunition. Rachel, you're getting food and medical supplies. I'm going for equipment and batteries. Meet back here in twenty minutes. Don't kill anyone unless they spot you. We're not equipped to get bogged down here," I whispered to the three of them through my microphone.

They all nodded and each signaled with a thumbs-up. "Good luck, ladies," Rachel joked as we all split up to accomplish our tasks.

I ran down a deserted street, jimmying my way into a convenience store where I began stuffing my bag with radios and batteries. I then took one last quick glance around; I spotted two hunting vests, which I tied to my backpack. As I emerged back into the street, a light made its way down.

I ducked into an alley, praying in silence that the fiends hadn't spotted me; it passed. A moment later voices of an enemy patrol passed by, talking in their foreign tongue. I was about to leave when suddenly the street became full of life. There were fiends running all over the street now, yelling at each other as tanks and helicopters started to circle Dublin.

"What the hell? Were you guys compromised?" I whispered into the headset, tucking myself into the safety of the shadows.

"No," came the replies of all three of my partners.

"Someone had to have ratted us out, Lance." Grant's voice said through my headset.

"Are you guys clear of the city?" I whispered back.

"Yeah, we're in the wood line," Grant replied.

"Go back to camp. I'll meet you there," I told him.

"No! I'm not leaving you here," Rachel yelled through her headset.

"Just go. I'm a big boy; I'll be fine," I told her.

She began to object, so I turned my headset off and shoved it into my backpack. I peeked through the back door where I discovered two fiends having a smoke and talking in human form. Pulling out my pistol, I griped the silencer to make sure it was on tight before shooting them each in the head and dragging their bodies into the store unseen by the enemy.

I sprinted down an ally but was forced to dive into another convenience store by the sight of three fiends and a tank rounding the corner. They immediately opened fire. I heard the thunderous roar of fiends as they flew above in an attempt to pinpoint my location.

The walls around started to break as the tank fired another round into the store. One fiend flew in, breaking through the window. I unloaded my full pistol clip into him. He snarled at me as he lay on the ground in a pool of his own blood before succumbing to his wounds.

I shouldered my sniper and shot him in the head to finish him off. Gripped by fear, I made my way to the back door where I unwittingly found a hidden cellar; its location had been kept secret by a rug. I could feel my insides jump for joy as I quickly opened the back door to make it look as though I had escaped and then tucked away in the safety of the cellar.

Waiting in silence, I listened to fiends rush inside, opening fire with assault rifles on nothing. They cursed and then ran through the back door. I poked my head out of the cellar, spotting one fiend standing guard near the dead fiend.

His eyes widened in fear as he spotted me aiming the pistol at his head. I squeezed the trigger, nothing happened.

He yelled for help fumbling to unsling his weapon as I tried to fire the pistol again, forgetting that I hadn't reloaded it. "Son of a—!" I yelled, throwing the pistol at him.

I ducked behind the counter as he opened fire on me with his assault rifle and ducked behind a fallen table. Calmly, I reached for my timber wolf. He continued to fire at the counter, breaking all the glasses above me.

"Put your hands up, filthy human," he yelled, pausing to reload.

I popped up with the sniper and shot him point-blank in the head. "No thanks," I replied.

He groaned, slumping lifelessly against the table. I picked up the pistol that I had thrown at him before putting it in my side pouch. I then loaded his assault rifle, shouldered my weapons, and ran through the abandoned hallway and out the front door.

I took shelter in an abandoned garbage can about five blocks down from where I had killed the fiend, closing the lid before curling up under the bags. The stench of the trash was unbearable, but that was the least of my worries. I was lulled to sleep by the swooshing sounds of fiend wings overhead who searched tirelessly for me all night.

When I awoke the next morning, there were no longer fiends or helicopters flying around. The streets had gone eerily quiet, absent of regular enemy patrols. I hopped out of the garbage can and sprinted into the woods, crashing straight into a tree.

My nose started to bleed, but I couldn't help laughing at myself in disbelief that I had survived all that unscathed just to be taken out by a tree. The walk back to camp was long and hard. I was so hungry and thirsty, but I kept going, finally bursting into the opening at our main gate.

"Freeze," the guard yelled, pointing his weapon at me. I put my hands up obediently and dropped to the ground. "Lance?" he asked, getting closer.

"The one and only," I replied with a smirk.

"Man, I heard what happened. Here, have a drink," he offered, holding out his canteen.

I thankfully took the water, wiping the blood from my face. "Did Rachel, Grant, and Ellie make it back safely?" I asked.

He nodded. I shot him a thankful smile as he helped me back up to my feet and led me into the camp. It was still morning, so the base was practically like a ghost town.

I trudged up a hill and entered the camp's headquarters hut. "Squad Leader Foxtrot reporting for debriefing, sir," I said, standing at the door and giving Captain Murphy a salute.

"Lance! We thought you were dead. Please have a seat, my boy," he said, gesturing toward the chair while pouring a glass of rum.

"Thank you, sir," I replied, graciously taking a sip of it.

"So go on. Explain to me what happened out there," he insisted, sitting back in his chair.

"Well, everything was going good until right at the end when the fiends somehow got wind that we were there, even though none of my men had been compromised. Rachel, Ellie, and Grant were all able to escape, but I got bogged down in the city overnight until this morning when the fiends left. I took out four of them, though, sir."

"Well, it's good to see you're all right. Alpha was massacred last night," he informed me as he took a drink.

"But how?" I questioned. "They were only doing a reconnaissance mission."

"The fiends ambushed them on the cliff that they were setting up their outpost on," he replied simply.

"Adam and Wight?" I asked.

"Both killed. I'm sorry, Lance. I know you were close to them."

I gulped with a nod, trying my best to fight back tears.

"There has to be a rat." I muttered in disbelief.

Captain Murphy nodded coming over to my side where he placed a reassuring hand on my shoulder. "Don't worry, Lance. We will flush him out, and when we find him, he will pay."

# CHAPTER 6

M Y MIND WAS RACING with thoughts as I walked along the camp up the rocky path to our cave, but I had to put them aside. There were more important issues to address. As I entered our shelter it was to the sight of Rachel sitting in the corner of the cave crying.

I walked over and silently sat down beside her, putting my hand around her shoulder. She gasped as she looked over at me. "You're alive!" she cried out, throwing her hands around me.

"Of course I'm alive," I replied with a grin.

She smothered me with kisses. "You're hurt," she told me as she looked down at the cuts along my arm. She gently swept her hand across my face, kissing me again.

"Yeah, I'm going to go get it checked out by Tina soon," I told her as I stood up.

"Here, take off your gear. I'll clean your weapons for you," she told me.

I obeyed, laying all my stuff down. I then kissed her forehead before leaving the cave.

"You look like shit," Tina told me as she sat me down and began taking pieces of glass out of my wounds. When she was done, she carefully washed them out with soap and water to kill any infections.

"It's nice to see you too." I said, cringing as she poured more water on my wounds.

Tina giggled, telling me to wait there as she went to get Kate who appeared around the corner of the medical hut a moment later. She and Tina, not wanting to fight, had taken the next best option and become medics at our field hospital. Kate, of course, being the stud that she was when it came to work, climbed the ladders quickly and was now the head medic for our camp.

She came in and knelt down beside me, examining my wounds. "You'll be fine," Kate assured me. "Your wounds will heal nicely, and your nose isn't broken."

"Good to know," I muttered. I could see the worry in her eyes.

"I thought you were going to take it easy for a bit," she noted.

I shrugged. "It was only a supply mission. I didn't think anything would happen."

She patted me on the shoulder "Something always happens around here, Lance," she whispered.

I shrugged again. "I made it out. It's not a big deal."

That was clearly not what she wanted to hear. "Get up," she ordered me.

"Huh?"

"I said, get up!" she yelled, grabbing hold of my arm and hauling me to my feet like a child. Kate led me to the next room, storming past cots of injured soldiers and coming to a rest at a curtain. As she opened, it I couldn't help but look away. An unconscious soldier was lying on the cot; his body mutilated by claw marks; both legs and his right arm were missing. The only finger the fiends had left on his remaining hand was the pinky.

"He was rescued by Charlie from a village south of here," Kate began.

"I don't think rescued is the proper word," I muttered, cutting her off.

She nodded her agreement. "His name is Clancy. I went to school with him before the war. He had been missing for two days. That's all the time the fiends needed to torture him, interrogate him, and then leave him for dead. Do you see what I'm saying, Lance? This isn't a game. Once you get caught, it's over—no ifs, ands, or buts about it."

I was speechless. Luckily, a sound forced us both to glance at the main door as an injured soldier came in nursing his arm. Kate glanced back to me and then strode away to attend to the soldier. I watched as both Kate and Tina helped him lie down on a cot.

After debating whether to say good-bye, I ended up just leaving, figuring it was easier for the three of us that way. Once I was outside, I immediately began heading to the basketball court. That visit with Kate had left a sour taste in my mouth, but there was still one more person I needed to visit.

I picked up a basketball and threw it at Grant's back. "Hey, asshole, get my ball," I yelled at him.

"Listen, you picked the wrong day to mess with me. I'm going to kick your ass, punk," Grant yelled, whirling around with a punch unaware that it was me. I ducked; he missed and then stood there, staring at me in disbelief.

His expression of anger instantly turned to joy. "You made it!" he exclaimed.

I nodded with a smirk.

"You down for a game?" he asked.

I pointed to my beat-up face. "Does it look like it?"

He laughed. "I've got to head back up anyway," I added. "Rachel was really worried about me."

"What? I get no love? I was worried about you to bro!" he joked, spreading his arms.

"Yeah, whatever. Get out of here," I replied with a friendly push as he went in for a hug.

Once I returned to the cave, I discovered Rachel happily cleaning my timber wolf. "You don't have to do that," I told her. "I'm just going to end up getting it dirty tonight anyway."

"I want to," she replied, her voice still quivering.

I opened up the envelope, reading our new mission to myself stumbling over some of the wording.

"What is it?" she asked.

"An ambush," I told her, folding it back up before placing the note into my pocket.

"What kind of an ambush?" she asked confused.

I usually wasn't so brief with her about our missions. "I can trust you to keep a secret, right?" I asked her.

She returned the stare, adding a gentle smile. "Of course you can, Lance."

I paused and let out a sigh. There was nothing I could keep from Rachel; we were basically one person. "Murphy and I think there's a rat in the camp selling information to the fiends," I explained to her. "You've got to keep that under wraps, though. If it leaks outside these walls, he will stop," I begged her.

She nodded, patting my arm reassuringly. "You're going to find him, right?"

I nodded confidently.

"I know you will," she whispered, sharing the same confidence. She tilted her head, leaning it against mine as we cuddled affectionately. "So what are we ambushing?" she asked with a casual shrug as we intertwined our hands.

"We've got to take out two supply trucks carrying weapons and some other munitions," I explained.

"Sounds easy," she replied.

"Yeah, let's hope so," I muttered, handing her the pay from the previous night's mission.

As night set in Rachel and I headed out to the rendezvous point to meet Grant and Ellie, who were five minutes late. I gave them an angry stare as they finally arrived, crashing through the thick foliage. "Sorry," Grant whispered, obviously out of breath.

"What the hell, guys? This isn't a drop-in center, you can't just show up whenever you feel like it," I snapped at them.

Ellie offered an apologetic shrug. I let out an angry sigh and motioned for everyone to follow me as we rushed to a dirt road which then lead to a main road that was a main supply route for Dublin, located thirty minutes from our camp. We arrived to the location just in time for Ellie to run out onto the road and set up a few explosives.

"All right, fan out; good luck," I muttered.

I gave Rachel a loving pat on the back. She glanced back with a wink before jogging down the road in search of a firing position. I perched myself in a tree about thirty-five meters from the ambush point.

It began to drizzle as we waited for the convoy to arrive. I checked through my scope to make sure that everyone was in position. Rachel was on the right side of the road loading her MP5; Grant was lying down on the left side of the road behind a dirt mound with his machine gun set up. Ellie was on the left side with Grant about fifteen meters away from him with a loaded rocket-propelled grenade launcher on her shoulder.

As time dragged on longer and longer, I started to have doubts that the convoy was even going to show up. But, sure enough, a few more minutes passed by when suddenly a pair of headlights broke the tranquility of the night's air. A Humvee rounded the corner followed by two trucks and another Humvee in the rear.

I shot the driver of the first one followed by the gunner on the turret of the vehicle. It swerved out of control and off the road before crashing into a tree and coming to a rest, leaving the two supply trucks vulnerable. They panicked, pressing on the gas in an attempt to escape but exploded on impact with the roadside bombs Ellie had set up.

From his mound, Grant opened fire at the second supply truck. The rear Humvee rounded the corner to join the fight and began spraying wildly into the mound Grant was taking cover behind, forcing him to cower back behind it. Ellie peeked from her position and fired the rocket-propelled grenade, which sailed through the air and hit the remaining Humvee dead on.

Grant ceased fire as Rachel and Ellie ran out onto the road and opened the doors of the four destroyed vehicles spraying bullets into them, taking no prisoners. The girls then threw grenades into the back of the supply truck before racing back to the safety of the edge of the road, thereby blowing up what remained of the ammunition inside. All in all, it was a picture-perfect mission.

The four of us ran back into the woods together, avoiding being spotted as the roaring engines of aircrafts could be heard arriving to aid the vehicles. Twenty-five minutes later, the four of us made it back to camp, mission complete. We trudged through the camp exhausted, but our spirits were high.

When we arrived at the outdoor bar later that night happy to be alive, everyone cheered for us as we sat down, congratulating us for successfully completing the mission. "Drinks are on us," the bartender called over, bringing us each a glass of whatever we wanted.

"Cheers for making it back to fight another day," Ellie said, holding up her glass.

We all clinked our glasses together. Rachel, Ellie, and Grant all started chatting excitedly, while I leaned back in my chair and quietly sipped my drink. The three of them sat there gloating about how easily they had killed the fourteen fiends to everyone who came to sit with us and congratulate us.

By the end of the night, everyone was hammered so I helped Grant, Ellie, and Rachel back to their shelters, not wanting them to injure themselves. I couldn't afford to have any of them to be forced to sit out of whatever our next mission would be.

"See you tomorrow, Lance!" Grant called over to us. Ellie, who was probably the most sober out of the three of them, helped him to there shelter.

"See ya, man," I called back as I picked up Rachel, who was passed out beside a tree.

It was a nice night out. The crickets chirped peacefully as I walked up the rocky dirt path to our shelter with Rachel in my arms. I blew up our air mattress, making my bed and then laying her on it before snuggling beside her. She opened an eye groggily with a smirk and snuggled closer to me as we absorbed each other's warmth.

When I woke up the next morning, Rachel was already up and cradling her head as she drank a glass of water. "What's up?" I asked with a laugh sitting up beside her.

"I feel like shit," she muttered with a smirk.

"I wonder why, Hun."

"Shut up." She giggled.

Later that morning, I went down to the camp's headquarters while Rachel got dressed and nursed her hangover. I could tell Captain Murphy was in an exceptionally good mood by the smile stained to his face as I entered.

"Aw, Lance, come in, come in. Sit, my boy," he offered, cheerfully waving toward the chair in front of his desk.

I accepted his offer and sat down as he did the same across the desk from me. "You and your troops did a fine job with that ambush last night," he complimented me, giving me an envelope filled with money.

"Thank you, sir," I replied.

He then took out some cash from his pocket and made four separate piles of three hundred dollars each. "I'm putting your squad on bivouac duties for three days. It'll be a good time for you guys to get some rest and relaxation," Captain Murphy added with a smile.

"Thank you, sir," I repeated, pausing for a moment. "What exactly are we resting for, though, sir—if you don't mind me asking?"

"Alpha and Echo are going to be sent on a two-month tour to Dublin to support other companies around these areas in retaking Dublin," he told me, handing the four stacks of money to distribute to my members.

"So you need us to fight for Dublin?" I asked.

He shook his head. I stared at him in confusion. He began again. "I have a more important mission for you four; hopefully, it will change the war once and for all," he confided in me.

My eyes lit up to the sounds of this. "What is it, sir?"

"You will know when the time comes," he told me with a firm nod.

I could tell he was dismissing me, so I nodded in agreement, obediently stood up, and saluted him before leaving the building and walking up to our den. When I arrived, I glanced around. Seeing that Rachel wasn't there, I tucked the money safely away in my sleeping bag.

I grabbed my bathing suit and soap and headed down to the lake were I figured Rachel was probably washing. "Hey there, sexy," she called, swimming over to me as I approached the side of the lake and set my stuff down.

"What's up?" I muttered, squatting down at the edge and feeling the lukewarm water.

"It's nice. Come in!" she invited. "So what did Grandpa have to say?" she asked with a giggle, referring to Captain Murphy.

I quickly jumped in and swam over to her side. "We're on general duties for three days," I told her, leaving out the Dublin assault.

"Sweet. It's about time we got a break!" she told me happily as we treaded water, the sun beaming off us gently.

Once we were done, we ended up coming to a rest at the basketball court, sitting down on the bleachers, and waiting for Ellie and Grant. We remained silent and listened to the birds happily chirping in the background. The birds were soon replaced by the dull sounds of the camp slowly coming to life—people waking up and beginning their daily duties.

"'Sup?" Grant called over. He and Ellie sauntered toward us, happily holding hands.

"Nothing much," I said, greeting him with our usual handshake as they sat down next to us on the bleachers. I pulled out the envelope of money I had received from Captain Murphy for our last mission, splitting it between the four of us.

"So Murphy put us on bivouac duties for three days as a reward for our hard work," I told them, leaning back on the railing of the bleachers as the sun beamed down on me.

"Awesome. So we basically just get to keep the generators running, collect resources, and stuff like that?" Ellie asked.

I nodded lazily. "I'm going to go hunting in a bit if anyone wants to come," I offered them, already knowing the answer as I saw Grant and Ellie share a disinterested look.

"I'll come!" Rachel volunteered.

I smiled thankfully. She returned it with a playful wink, as I mouthed the words "thank you" to her.

"So you guys are going to hold things down around here while we're gone?" I asked, turning my attention to Ellie and Grant.

They nodded; their disinterest was clear as they basked in the warm morning sun. "You guys want to do something tonight?" Ellie offered Rachel and I as we got up to leave.

"Sure," we both agreed.

Rachel and I made our way up the path to our squad's shelter, where I grabbed my loyal timber wolf sniper rifle.

I put a sling on it while patiently waiting for Rachel to get her hunting kit prepared, as we'd be departing a short time later. We walked along the woods, occasionally stopping to allow Rachel time to set up her traps and a few snares in some good escape routes for rabbits. After about twenty minutes of walking, we found a nice place on a mountaintop, overlooking a valley below us, about eight hundred meters away.

I set up my timber wolf on the ridge and glanced through the sight down at the valley.

"This is a beautiful spot," Rachel commented, pulling out her binoculars.

She surveyed the layout of the ground, doing her job, which I had already done for her. "I'd say that's about eight hundred meters to a kilometer, by the way, Lance."

I nodded, having already finished the calculations for the shot in my head. A few minutes passed by as I stared through the sight, patiently waiting for a deer to wander into the valley below.

"Geez, it's going be a long day if you plan on doing that," Rachel joked.

I smirked, setting the butt of the sniper rifle down on the ground. I could tell something was on her mind. A silence passed between us for a moment until Rachel finally said, "Do you remember what life was like before the war?"

"Not really," I told her honestly.

"Yeah, me either," she muttered, pausing for a second to look at me then tearing her eyes away back to the valley. "I was trying to go through my memories of my life before the war the other day, and nothing was coming up. I can't even see my parents' faces anymore."

I didn't say anything; there was nothing I really could

say. If I did speak, it would just upset her even more. "I suppose it's not all bad, though. If it weren't for this war, I would have never met you," she told me, a faint smile spreading across her face.

I returned her compliment with a pat on the back; she gave me a peck on the cheek before shifting her attention back to the valley. I let out a relaxed sigh, glancing at the afternoon sun off in the distance, the silhouettes of mountains almost seeming painted into the background.

"I wish the fiends would just hurry up and lose this war," Rachel said to herself, breaking the tranquil silence that had set in around us.

She took her hair band out to let her long, blonde hair drape down her back as we lay there motionless. "Do you think we're going to win?" she asked.

"Honestly?" I asked. "I don't think we are going to be around to find that out, Rachel." Her smile faded away in disappointment. "Besides, there are no winners in war. Wars are just fought to pave the road to a political solution—in this case, who gets which parts of the world when all this fighting is said and done."

She remained silent; I knew that was not the answer she was looking for, but it was the only one I could give without lying.

"Well, that's cheery, Lance," she finally said.

"It's realistic. Look around—it's been three years now, Rachel, and I've still seen no progress by the People's Liberation Force."

"What's wrong with you?" she asked quietly after a few minutes.

"Huh?" I said, confused.

"You've been so distant over the past few days," she told me, inching a little closer to me in an attempt to cuddle.

"I'm sorry; I'm just tired of this," I said, feeling emotionless. "I guess I'm just fed up of hiding in these dam woods. I want my old life back, that's all."

"It will come," she promised with a kiss.

We lay there for a couple hours, offering idle conversation now and then as we waited patiently for a deer to unknowingly wander into our path. Then our opportunity finally came. "It's about time," I grunted, shouldering my sniper rifle to peer through the scope as a full-grown doe wandered out into the open meadow below and began to peacefully graze on the grass.

"Nine hundred meters," Rachel whispered.

I grunted my thanks, keeping my breathing steady as I adjusted for the calculations of the shot on my sight. My finger was on the trigger, and I was about to squeeze when suddenly a baby fawn galloped from the wood line into the meadow, coming to a rest at its mother's side. I let out an unhappy sigh, allowing my breathing to return to normal as I set the butt of the weapon back down on the ground glancing over at Rachel who was staring at me with a look of confusion on her face.

"What's wrong, Lance?" she asked.

"I'm not going to kill its mother," I whispered firmly, staring back out to the meadow.

She glanced back out to the field before she looked back at me and sent me a smile of approval. "You've got a heart of gold."

I returned her smile with a faint one, got up from my prone position, and started packing up my gear. "Hopefully we got a few rabbits with the snares," I noted.

She nodded in agreement as we finished up. Luckily, we did end up catching five rabbits in the eight traps Rachel had set up, so we didn't go back to camp empty-handed. Our contribution was pretty pitiful compared to all the other hunting parties who had shown up with deer, but at least it was better than nothing.

"Wow, nice catch!" someone called from behind me as Rachel and I arrived at the meal hall to skin our rabbits.

I glanced back and spotted Brent observing us with a playful grin smeared across his face. Per usual, he was scratching his goatee.

"Brent!" Rachel squeaked excitedly, throwing her hands in the air and running over to him to give him a hug.

"Shut up, man. I can't believe they let your ugly mug back into these parts of the woods," I called over to him, unable to contain myself from smiling due to his return.

He laughed as he made his way around the table, Rachel still wrapped around him. "So what's up with you? It looks like you lost a good twenty pounds out west," she complimented him, finally letting Brent go.

"Not much. There's less beer over there," he told us with a laugh. "What's up with you, girl?"

"Oh, you know how it is—one of those days," she replied, returning her attention to skinning the rabbits.

"I can see that," Brent noted.

The three of us laughed, and he joined in to help us skin the rabbits. "So I hear you're Foxtrot's squad leader," he said.

"Yeah, the one and only," I muttered with a smirk.

He laughed. "You guys sure did grow up fast, and it's only been what? One or two years?"

I shrugged. "Yeah, something like that. Things change in a minute's notice around here, though."

Brent nodded in agreement. "Need an M203 in your squad?" he asked.

I laughed. "You're kidding, right? You want to join? Murphy will probably just give you Alpha back," I told him.

He gave an uninterested shrug toward the thought of being back in charge of Alpha. "It's not the real Alpha anymore; besides, I don't want to ruffle any feathers around here."

"Well, you're going to regardless nowadays, man," I warned him. "Everyone thinks he's a superstar around here."

Brent laughed. "Looks like we're going to have to start putting some kids in their place then," he promised as he handed over the last skinned rabbit.

"Sounds like a plan," I said with a thankful nod.

"Did you need anything else?" he asked.

"Nah, man. Thanks for the help. We'll catch you later," I called to him, handing the skinned rabbits to the cooks.

"Doubt you'll be catching anything by the looks of today's catch," he called back.

I laughed to myself as I grabbed Rachel's hand and tossed him the middle finger with the other as the three of us parted ways. Rachel and I headed up the hill to our cave.

"You did a good thing today, Lance. I'm proud of you," Rachel reminded me once we got into our cave and had set all our gear down.

"Thanks. Make sure to tell that to all the hungry people

tonight," I replied with a laugh, giving her a hug as I began to take my sniper rifle apart and clean the firing mechanism.

Rachel followed suit, sitting down beside me and taking her own weapon apart. We cleaned in silence for a little while until Rachel chirped up again. "I hear Captain Murphy's throwing a bonfire tonight for the troops."

"Really?" I asked, glancing up from my weapon.

She smiled, sending me a nod. "Did you want to go?"

"For sure," I said, my spirits lifting already by the news.

"Awesome," she replied, placing a kiss on my cheek as I returned to cleaning my timber wolf.

The bonfire was pretty amazing. The smell of meat and the sound of laughter as we approached the party was a clear indication that it was going to be a good night. I had a great time with Rachel and the gang. Grant, Ellie, Rachel, Brent, and I were some of the first to arrive. We dug into the cleaned meat the cooks laid out and began roasting our portions over the fire.

"Hey, man, I heard that you and Rachel had the catch of the day," a familiar voice called over to me.

I glanced up from the fire to see Jessie, which was no surprise. Anywhere Brent went, Jessie wasn't far behind. "It is what it is," I called over to him with a shrug as he came to our side. He greeted me with a fist bump before saying hi to the others.

Once we were done eating, there was a wave of people shushing one another as Captain Murphy stood up to address us all. "Good evening," Captain Murphy called out to us.

"Good evening, sir," we all called back followed by a mass wave of applause.

He smiled, raising his hands up slightly to douse the cheers and then cleared his throat. "I brought you all here tonight as a treat. I know it's been a rough last couple of months. We've lost many good men and women, but the fiends have suffered twice that number. We have pulled through in holding our ground, and the fiends now know that the Harush Forest is not up for grabs." His words sparked more cheers and chanting.

"You should all be very proud of yourselves," he added once the cheers started to subside again. "You are now a part of history. Your children, your grandchildren, your great-grandchildren, and their great-grandchildren are all going to read about your noble efforts in this region. So with that being said, everyone enjoy your night off, because it's time to get wasted!" He triumphantly lifted a beer that a soldier handed him.

We all cheered for a final time as some volunteers came out with trays of free beer. Everyone did the mad scramble to grab their four free beers for the night. I glanced back to see Lieutenant Stark off to the side.

He was dimly lit by the fire, and I could see his arms folded across his chest and a sombre expression painted across his face. There was a blond man beside him sharing the same expression. Lieutenant Stark whispered something into the man's ear, and the blond then nodded before leaving out of sight.

Stark was joined by Captain Murphy a moment later. They exchanged what appeared to be a few heated words to one another, and then Stark stormed off. My mind was instantly jarred away from the incident as Rachel happily turned my head to face her as we began to make out on the log we were perched on, our shadows dancing off the fire as the night carried on.

Rachel and Ellie got a little too drunk as usual, so once it was time to leave, Grant and I picked them up. We nodded our good nights to one another and went our separate ways to our sleeping accommodations. I set Rachel down and rested her against a bolder covered over with moss as I blew up our air mattresses and made our bed for the night.

She stared at me affectionately as I finished. "What are you grinning at, silly?" I asked, returning her silly grin as I took off my shirt and pants, stripping down to my boxers before going over to her resting spot and retrieving her.

I then gently placed her on the air mattresses. "You.... You're so cute." She giggled drunkenly and gave me a kiss as I helped her take off her clothes and get ready for bed.

She stared at me affectionately while taking off her bra. "What are you doing?" I asked.

"Come on. You know we can't fool around, Rachel. Captain Murphy would kill us if he found out. No sex until the war is over—that's the rule," I reminded her.

"I know," she said innocently. "I just want to keep you warm; that's all." She giggled as she laid down and snuggled close to me. I instantly felt the warmth from her bare chest as she wrapped her arms around me affectionately.

"You're drunk," I reminded her with a smirk.

She giggled. "So are you."

"Good night, Rachel."

"Good night, sexy."

I smiled before blowing out the flickering candle in our den. I rested my head against hers, the two of us peacefully drifting off.

# Chapter 7

THE NEXT MORNING I was summoned by a runner to Captain Murphy's hut. "What do you think he wants?" Rachel asked.

All I had to offer was a shrug; I was just as clueless as she was. I let out a dull yawn, muttering some profanity to myself as I searched around the den for my hunting uniform, which was what we would wear during work. It was a beautiful morning out with a cool July breeze making the grass flow back and forth as if it had a life of its own.

"Good morning, sir," I greeted Captain Murphy at the door, giving him a salute.

He smiled warmly, returning the salute before finishing off his smoke. "Come on in. We have a lot to talk about," he told me, motioning toward the door.

The two of us walked in and settled down at his desk. I could tell it was something important as he pulled out a file containing a whole bunch of pictures. He stared at it before setting it down on the desk and turning it for me to see.

"Dublin, sir?" I asked, staring at the pictures of rubble.

"That's right," he replied, turning the folder back around toward himself.

"You grew up there, didn't you?" he muttered, still staring at the folder.

I nodded and found myself deep in thought as memories of my previous life came flooding in. "I'm sending your team in to perform the public execution of one of the highest value targets we've ever had. The shot is not to be taken until the speech is over. Understand?" he asked me.

I nodded, having already expected something like this to happen. "When?" I asked simply.

"Tomorrow," he replied, matching my tone.

"I have full confidence in you, son. We're going to change this war around," he promised me.

"Yes, sir," I muttered. I could tell something was on his mind. "What is it?" I asked him as we transferred to a more casual conversation.

"It's nothing really; you know, you four kids are like my own." I get nervous every time Foxtrot goes out, because I don't ever want to see you guys come back with the news that one of you has been killed," he admitted as he sat back in his chair and poured himself a glass of rum. He offered me a sip, which I accepted gratefully.

"I'll do my best to make sure we all come home together," I promised him.

He nodded. "I know you will, Lance. I'm sure you are already aware that Jessie and Brent are back. They requested to be placed in your squad."

I nodded.

"Would that be all right?" he asked.

"Of course," I replied without hesitation.

"Then it's settled." He reached into the folder and handed me my orders. "All the information's right there. If you have any questions, my doors are always open."

I nodded as I stood up to shake his hand good-bye. Thankfully, by the time that I got back up to the den, Rachel had everything all sorted out and the bed all packed away.

"What did Murphy want?" she asked as I sat down on the edge of a bolder, glancing over to her with a dull grin.

"We got a tour to Dublin," I told her.

"No way!" she exclaimed, snatching the papers from my hands to read over them. "Wow," She finally muttered after looking them over.

I nodded my head in agreement.

"Do the others know?" she asked.

"Not yet," I responded. "Brent and Jessie are in our squad now."

"Excellent—not saying you can't handle anything that's thrown our way, but it's always good to have experience working on your side," she told me.

I nodded, holding out my hand and grasping hers as the two of us walked down to the basketball court where our usual squad's meeting took place. Sure enough, Grant, Ellie, Brent, and Jessie were sitting there waiting for us.

"What's up, playa?" Grant called to me as the crew spotted us approaching.

"Not much. Just got our orders from Murphy," I called back to him, casually taking a seat on the bleachers beside them, Rachel by my side.

"Anything exciting?" Ellie asked.

"Not really ... besides that were leaving camp tomorrow on a nice scenic hike to Dublin for a mission," I replied, a dull grin spreading across my face.

"Get out of here with that bullshit!" Brent called to me in disbelief.

The four of them sat there looking at me flabbergasted.

I laughed as I handed them the orders I had received from Murphy. "Well, I guess we better get packing, huh?" Jessie muttered in his usual noninterest tone.

I nodded in agreement, finishing off my squad's usual morning meeting.

"Well, I think they took the news well." Rachel said as we walked back up the path to our den.

"Yep," I muttered.

"What's wrong?" she asked.

"It's nothing really; just ... well ... if something happens to me out there, I want you to leave me okay? Don't worry about anything but keeping yourself safe, all right?" I asked her.

"Bu—" she began.

"Promise me," I insisted, cutting her off.

She stared at me for a moment before finally agreeing. "I promise," she whispered, interweaving her fingers with mine as we reached our shelter.

"Thank you," I replied.

I knew she was just telling me what I wanted to hear, but at least it settled my worries about her safety for the time being. "Don't even think about stuff like that, Lance. It's going to be a cakewalk anyway," Rachel called over to me as we packed our gear and prepared for the next day.

"An assassination in the heart of Dublin is no cakewalk," I said, not wanting her to take our mission lightly.

She shrugged, doing up her straps. As she finished packing all her kit, she turned her attention to her weapon. I didn't spend much time packing, knowing that regardless of how well we packed, we would run out of supplies in the city and be forced to restock ourselves from abandoned stores.

We met Ellie, Grant, Brent, and Jessie at sunrise the next morning. The mood was somber; we exchanged reassuring smiles with one another, remaining silent as we waited for Bravo to meet up with us. I glanced at my watch, taking note that they were running late.

A few minutes later there was rustling in the bushes, and Bravo's leader, Alex, emerged from the dense foliage surrounding the rock where we had all agreed to meet. Alex was the newest squad leader in the camp, a slim guy in his late twenties with a Mohawk that would make you keel over laughing at.

"What's up?" I asked, glancing at his lack of kit. All he had was a half-packed backpack and his sidearm strapped to his leg.

"Um, is this a joke? Where's your squad, bro?" I asked him, both annoyed and confused by the delay.

"Sorry, man, we just received orders from Lieutenant Stark to stand down until thirteen hundred hours," he explained to me.

"Huh?"

Alex gave me a shrug. "Murphy and Stark are having a spat about the mission."

I let out an angry sigh. "I don't have time for this," I muttered to myself.

"Foxtrot Six One, this is Sunray Minor; message, over." Stark's voice came through the radio calling for me.

"Foxtrot Six One. Send," I said into the headset.

"Sunray Minor, the scheduled departure time has been amended to thirteen hundred hours; acknowledge," he told me.

"Foxtrot Six One, acknowledged." I muttered angrily,

turning to my squad and nodding for them to follow me back to base.

"What's going on?" Rachel asked, sounding just as confused as I was.

"No clue. I'm going to go sort this mess out right now," I grunted as we arrived back to camp.

I glanced around the camp and witnessed everyone fit for fighting getting geared up in their kits, looking as if we were going to launch a massive assault on Dublin in an attempt to take it by force.

"I don't know what the hell's going on. Stay here, guys; kit down. I'll be right back," I ordered my squad, shouldering the timber wolf before jogging up to headquarters.

I walked in uninvited, greeted by the sight of Captain Murphy and Lieutenant Stark yelling back and forth across the table at each other. Both men looked like rabid dogs with foam forming around their mouths. Both men's faces were red as an apple. Their attention immediately shifted to me as the door creaked closed.

I gulped, wishing I were a fly on the wall, knowing this was not a good time at all to find out what was going on. "This isn't a dam walk-in clinic. Get the hell out!" Stark yelled at me.

"Don't you ever talk to my soldiers that way," Captain Murphy barked at him.

"Shut the fuck up, old man," came the rebuttal from Stark.

"Listen here, maggot. I've been around this business a hell of a lot longer than you. We're going through with the plan that is already set in motion," Captain Murphy commanded.

"No we're not. We're going to get all our troops together and take this damn city once and for all," Stark argued.

"What? And lose half of them in the process? Leave behind all the women and children to fend for themselves here at the camp? Are you crazy?" Captain Murphy tried to reason with him.

"They won't need this damn camp when they have a solid roof over their heads for the first time in half a decade," Stark continued passionately.

"We're going through with the plan as it stands," Murphy reiterated, ignoring Stark's statement.

"Well, you're not taking Bravo then. They're mine," Stark shot back.

"I'll send whoever the hell I feel like. This is my camp, not yours. I'm in charge, not you. Understand?" Captain Murphy yelled, placing his hand on his pistol holster to further set Lieutenant Stark in his place.

Silence enveloped the hut for a brief moment. I watched Stark glance from Murphy's hand to his face before finally swallowing his pride. "Your wish is my command, sir," he muttered with a sneer before giving Murphy a salute and storming out of the hut.

I glanced at Captain Murphy, whose hand timidly came off the pistol holster as if just waiting for bullets to start flying through the wooden frame of the hut at us. I was speechless. Murphy glanced at his watch and then stared out the window.

I followed his stare, seeing Rachel, Grant, Brent, and Jessie sitting on a log all geared up ready to go. Sure enough, I saw Alex and his men come over to my group and settle down waiting for me.

"You better get going," Murphy muttered. "The war isn't going to wait for us."

"Yes, sir," I replied, giving him a salute, which he returned.

"Make us proud out there, Lance," he ordered me.

"I will, sir," I promised, making my departure from the hut.

I jogged back down the dirt path from the headquarters to my squad where I was greeted by Alex. "Ready to get down to business?" he asked, offering me his hand.

I smiled and shook it, "You know it."

We got our guys to fan out in a single-file line walking along the path to Dublin with five-meter spacing between each of us. Dublin, formally known as Halifax, used to be my home growing up. It was now nothing but a pile of rubble that the fiends held onto out of spite just so that we couldn't have our homeland back.

It took us the entire day to reach the outskirts of the city. When we finally did reach the edge, Alex and I crawled up to the berm of the wood line and peered down into the city. Fiends were visible everywhere, flying around and conducting patrols.

Some were in human form, while others were not. The human-formed fiends were working on their weapons and vehicles, while others were just hanging around, eating, and joking with one another.

"I think we should move down west a little before we make our entry," I suggested to Alex.

He nodded in agreement. We moved about five hundred meters to the west and then peaked over the berm again, happy to see that it was clear. Everyone lined up against the edge, and then I raised my hand to signal the count—five, four, three, two, one. "Go, Go, Go, Go!" I ordered.

The twelve of us all got up and sprinted down the hill toward the city, making it without a shot being fired.

I held my hand up to signal a halt. We knelt against the wall for a few minutes listening for any signs of movement, but there were none. We had successfully made it into the city undetected.

"Seems clear," Alex told me, taking out his map to find his objective.

I did the same. "Well, looks like you got a few things to handle on your own," I told him.

He nodded in agreement with a shake of my hand. "I'll see you tomorrow morning for the extraction," he said.

I nodded, giving him one last confident smile before my team and I left toward our objective. It took us five gruelling hours to get there, filled with lots of detours and halts to avoid enemy patrols and sentries. "Time check," I whispered to Rachel as we reached the safety of a three-story building close to our objective.

"Two in the morning," she whispered.

I nodded, leading everyone into the beaten-up building. "Watch your step," I whispered back to them as we navigated ourselves through the rubble.

After five minutes, we reached the third story of the building. It appeared that the space had once been an office of some sort, probably a telemarketer business or something similar judging by all the destroyed cubicles. I grabbed a table and set it up by a shattered window, making sure I could see the parking lot below perfectly through the sight of my weapon. "You guys get some sleep. Jessie has first shift in two hours," I told them.

They all began to obediently take off their kits, talking among themselves in hushed whispers as they got ready for bed. I rested against the wall with my arms crossed, waiting for them to settle down. I watched Rachel in silence; she blew up her air mattress and then retrieved her sleeping bag, placing it on top.

It wasn't long after I had returned my gaze back out the shattered window that I felt Rachel's arm wrap around my waste. I sent her a smile, which she returned. Pulling out her canteen, Rachel took a sip. "Drink?" she offered, holding it out to me.

"No thanks, babe," I replied, shaking her offer away with my hand.

"Take it," she insisted. "I don't want you to go down from dehydration."

I let out a sigh and agreed to accept her offer by taking a sip from the canteen before handing it back. "Thanks," I whispered with an affectionate kiss to her forehead.

She nodded, tucking it away and rewrapping her arms around me. "Go get some sleep," I whispered.

"Fine. Love you," she whispered back.

"Love you too. Sweet dreams," I replied, giving her bum a little pat.

She giggled and then headed toward her sleeping bag to tuck herself in. As the room began to fill up with snores, I smiled, glancing back out the window to the empty streets below and praying to myself that the next day's events would change the tide of the war.

# Chapter 8

THERE WAS NO NEED to be woken up the next morning; the deafening sounds of tanks rolling by did a fine enough job on their own. Struggling to my feet still in a daze, I stumbled over to the window that Brent was staring out of. "What's going on out there?" I asked.

"Your guess is as good as mine," he grunted, stepping aside to let me peer through the window at the ground below.

I watched in disbelief as five tanks outside began to set up a perimeter around where the speech was suppose to take place. To make things worse, more than a hundred troops marched into the parking lot. The familiar whooshing of fiend wings began to fill the air around us as their patrols commenced.

There was a loud explosion as they blew a door off the building across from ours and about ten or fifteen fiends funnelled in, searching for any resistance fighters. "We need to move. They're securing the perimeter," I whispered to my guys.

As if on command, there was a loud explosion downstairs that resulted in the building quaking as the fiend's entered. The six of us scurried along the top floor being quiet as church mice in search of a back stairwell. We jogged down one flight of stairs, coming to a rest under the next pair of stairs where we crammed in like sardines.

We could hear the yells of fiends as they barked orders and commands to the troops in their foreign tongue. I glanced over to Ellie; her face was plastered with fear. All I could offer her was a wink and a faint smile; it seemed to do the job, though.

We huddled in the stairwell for close to an hour. Finally, the fiends' yells began to patter away before finally exiting the building. Everyone, including me, let out a thankful sigh.

"Thank God fiends don't do very thorough searches," Grant grunted.

There was a wave of agreement as the six of us struggled up to our feet, shaking out our stiff joints and then returning back to the top floor where we had taken shelter during the night.

I peered through the window and was greeted by the sight of other fiends beginning to gather down in the parking lot where they appeared to be erecting a podium for the ceremony. "It looks like things are about to get under way. Get everyone in their positions," I ordered with a glance to Brent.

He nodded, going over to the others and placing them around the room to secure it in case a patrol stumbled upon us. "Over here, Grant," I called, motioning him to the window beside mine.

"What's up?" he asked, confused as I let him take my spot in the window.

"After I take the shot, open up on them," I said.

He nodded and crouched beside the window. I then

motioned Rachel over; we met by the next window just as a limousine pulled up near the podium. The crowd outside turned silent. *"Atriation!"* a fiend yelled out to the crowed.

They all snapped to attention. Two men strolled over from the podium, one opening the door of the limousine. An older gentleman in his military uniform, chest filled with medals, emerged from the limo accompanied by five armed guards.

He shook the two men's hands politely before being escorted to the podium by his entourage. "Is he the man?" I whispered to Rachel while shouldering the sniper, watching the events unfold below in anticipation.

She retrieved a photo from her breast pocket, holding it out for the both of us to see. "General Zitrova, commander of all operations in and around the Harush Forest," she whispered to me with a glance from the photo to the man below.

"It's him," I whispered to her.

She nodded in agreement and tucked the picture back into her breast pocket. "He's got some set on him, showing his face around this area," Rachel grunted, pure disgust laced in her voice.

"It will be his first and last visit to Dublin," I promised her.

"Foxtrot Six One, this is Foxtrot Six Two. Do you have eyes on the target?" Alex's voice sprang to life on the radio.

"Foxtrot Six One, roger. Where are you?"

"Foxtrot Six Two, my location is the bombed-out café," Alex replied.

"Foxtrot Six One, roger. Engage on my shot," I told him.

"Foxtrot Six Two, roger," came the reply followed by static as radio silence kicked in.

General Zitrova reached for the microphone and pulled it close. A hush spread around the crowd. We waited patiently for his speech to conclude. Captain Murphy wanted it that way for some reason.

"What do you think he's saying?" Rachel asked.

"Blah-blah-blah, we're the best. Blab-la-blah, humans are bad. Blah-blab-la, we will kill them all," I grunted.

A smirk spread across her face. She was about to say something when a cheer rang out from the crowd outside. All the fiends threw their right fists in the air triumphantly, signalling what appeared to be the end of his speech.

"Time to end this," I muttered to Rachel, clicking off the safety of the timber wolf.

She grunted in agreement. "Two hundred meters, Lance."

I whispered my thanks and took aim through the scope. I let the crosshairs come to rest just above the bridge of the man's beaklike nose. I exhaled, and my finger closed around the trigger.

The shot rang out. A plume of red and gray erupted from the general's head. Zitrova's death was so fast that I don't think anyone had enough time to process it. There was a split second of awed silence immediately followed by panicked yells erupting as some scattered while others began looking for the origin of the shot.

"Open fire!" I yelled through my microphone.

Grant smashed out the window, spraying wildly at the parking lot below. "Open fire!" I repeated into the microphone, glancing at the café, which was mysteriously absent of muzzle flashes.

There was no reply. "Goddamn it," I mumbled.

I began firing out the window as the fiends zeroed in on our building. "Fall back!" I called to Grant realizing our building was a sitting duck with no covering fire from the café.

The building took a violent shake as it was pounded with the fire of tanks sending dust, concrete, and rubble flying everywhere. "Get out! This place is going to collapse," Brent yelled.

We made it out just in time, making it a hundred meters away before the building came crumbling to the ground behind us. I led my squad into an abandoned alleyway, placing a finger against my lips to signal for everyone to take cover. The six of us coward into the protection of the shadows as the ominous swooping sounds of fiends above passed by.

We stayed there for a good ten or fifteen minutes before creeping along the labyrinth of alleyways leading to the edge of Dublin. "Where are we?" Grant asked once we had made it back up into the wood line.

I shrugged. "A hell of a lot safer then we were before," I muttered, pulling out my map.

"That's for sure," Jessie grunted.

Ellie, Grant, and Rachel took up firing positions in the form of a perimeter as Brent, Jessie, and I stared at the map in search of our position. "Here we are," Brent finally muttered after five minutes of looking.

I stared at the spot he was pointing at unhappily, "We came out on the opposite side of the city," I grunted as I folded up the map. "Everyone, get that water into you. It's going to be a long hike back."

There was an unfamiliar feeling in the air when we arrived back at camp that night. I glanced around. There were no bonfires, no drunks wandering the camp, even the decks of huts were mysteriously absent of people joking amongst themselves. "Is it just me, or does something not feel right?" I whispered to the others.

"You're not the only one," I heard Grant mutter in the background.

Rachel, Ellie, and the others all grunted in agreement. We cautiously made our way to the headquarters hut to report to Captain Murphy, but instead we were greeted at the door by a pissed off Lieutenant Stark who came barreling through the door.

"Sir," I muttered, raising my hand to salute him.

He ignored us and continued to walk up the path out of sight. The door cracked open, revealing the flustered face of Captain Murphy. His expression instantly softened at the sight of us.

"Thank God you guys made it back all right." He greeted us, shaking each of our hands individually before gathering us into his hut.

"How did everything go in Dublin?" he asked once we had all found a spot to settle down.

"Well, um, I don't know what happened out there, sir, but Bravo never gave us covering fire. They must have been compromised or something, but we haven't seen them since."

After hearing the news, the troubled expression returned to Captain Murphy's face.

"Was the mission completed?" he asked

"Like taking candy from a baby," I replied.

"He's dead?"

"Yes, sir."

He sent me a halfhearted smile. "Very good. I will make sure Bravo is disciplined for their actions," he promised us.

I could tell his mind was preoccupied with other thoughts. "Is there something wrong, sir?" Rachel asked.

Captain Murphy let out a sigh with a nod of his head. Grant and I glanced at each other before returning our gaze back to him. Growing up, Captain Murphy was like the father we had never had, so to see him down in the dumps like this was probably harder on us then it was for him.

"I can trust you guys, right?" he finally asked.

"Of course," we all said.

He paused for a second as if debating whether he was going to tell us what was on his mind. "I need you kids to keep your ears open out there," he began.

"For what?" Ellie asked, saying what we were all thinking.

"Betrayals," he muttered coldly.

"Betrayals?" Rachel repeated, her eyebrow rising in interest.

Captain Murphy nodded. "Stark has been questioning my authority lately. I believe he is raising an army to attempt a mutiny.... It's a little shooting club that call themselves the NWO."

"Why would Stark do that?" Grant chimed in, confused.

"Power, of course," I muttered to myself loud enough for everyone to hear.

Captain Murphy grunted in agreement. "He thinks we should bring the fight to the fiend's front door and retake Dublin," Murphy explained.

"Shouldn't we though?" Grant asked.

I glanced over to him with a warning look, knowing that was not the answer Murphy wanted to hear. He glanced around at the six of us before clearing his throat. "Would you guys mind excusing Grant, Lance, and I for a minute?" Murphy asked.

"No problem, sir," Brent said.

"You can keep them," Ellie added, making us all laugh. Not even Captain Murphy could keep a straight face.

The girls came up to us to say their good-byes, giving us a kiss good night before taking their leave out the front door followed by Brent and Jessie. "Here. Take a seat, boys," Captain Murphy offered us once they had left, motioning to the two chairs in front of his desk.

We both did obediently; I had a kind of nervous feeling in my stomach as he quietly poured three glasses of rum. I found myself wondering what he wanted to speak to us about.

"So tell me, Grant, how many friends and family members have you lost to this war?" Captain Murphy asked, handing us each a glass of rum, which we sipped on silently.

"Too many," Grant replied.

I knew where this was heading.

"Exactly. We've all lost too many loved ones in this war, and I, for one, am tired of it. That's why with my strategy of guerrilla warfare, it's a win/win situation. We take minimum casualties and keep the fiends at bay in Dublin. Sooner or later, peace talks will start. A full-out offensive campaign against the fiends like Lieutenant Stark is proposing would do nothing but hinder the inevitable peace talks between us and the fiends," Captain Murphy explained.

I glanced over at Grant who was staring down at his cup in shame. All I could offer was a light pat on the back. Captain Murphy also shot him a light smile before taking a sip of his rum.

The approval of Captain Murphy's forgiveness for Grant's stupid question seemed to be all that was needed as he returned, it lighting up.

"Sir, forgive me, but aren't you scared that if we don't bring the fight to the fiends, they will bring the fight to us?" I asked him.

He shook his head, a confident smirk across his face. "It is a no brainer that occasionally they will send heavier waves of attacks into the Harush Forest in an attempt to smoke us out, but we will just fight harder and repel all their attacks until the day comes that they agree to a cease-fire." Murphy had answered my question.

I heard Grant mutter in agreement with Captain Murphy's answer so decided not to argue the point further, as our conversation began to veer off to less serious topics. "So how's everything going between you guys and the girls?" Murphy asked with a laugh.

We shrugged. "The usual," Grant spoke up for the both of us with a smirk.

Captain Murphy chuckled to himself as he topped off all our drinks. "It seems like just yesterday that this whole thing started. I remember I used to catch you kids all the time in so much trouble around camp, and now look at yourselves—young, mature men. You've both grown up so fast," He complimented us.

We both thanked him sincerely, but it was more of a sombre mood that was taking over the hut. It almost felt like he was saying his good-byes to us. "Well, boys, that's all I wanted to talk to you about. Do me proud out there," he told us.

I noticed he was getting a bit choked up. "We will, sir," we both promised him, shaking his hand before leaving.

By the time I had gotten back up to the cave, Rachel was sound asleep. Luckily for me, she had taken the time to blow up both of our air mattresses. I thankfully snuggled next to her, feeling the soft movements of her chest as she slept.

I couldn't help the smile spreading across my face as I let sleep finally over come me knowing everything would be fine. The next morning I was gently shaken awake by Rachel. "Good morning, sweetie," she said, greeting me with a kiss.

"Morning." I glanced over to my wristwatch, wiping away the sleep from my eyes to see that it was nine o'clock in the morning. She had let me sleep in.

My attention shifted back to her as she plopped down beside me and pulled out two apples from her pockets, offering me one for breakfast. "Thanks," I said, accepting the apple with a smile.

She returned the smile, and we began to eat in silence as I tried to plan out the day's events in my head. "So are you and Ellie going to try to work the girls a bit today for some information on what's been going on?" I asked Rachel as we finished eating.

"Yeah, what about you? Going to do some manly bonding today around camp?" she asked with a sarcastic flex of her arms.

I laughed. "Something like that," I said, giving her a playful shove.

"Captain Murphy didn't really give Grant and me much

information, but apparently the group we're looking for is called the NWO. They're a little club Lieutenant Stark has made." I told her.

"What does NWO stand for?"

"No clue," I told her truthfully.

She gave me a light smile, which I returned. I leaned over and gave her a kiss before getting ready to go meet up with Grant. It was a beautiful day out, but not even that seemed to brighten up the mood around camp. Everyone was working quietly. There was no friendly chatter being thrown around the camp, no one asking, "Hey, how's it going?" Even the basketball court was abandoned.

"It's like a funeral around here," Grant muttered to me. I grunted in agreement as we walked along the path toward the firing range where we could hear the distinct sounds of pistols being fired.

"Hey, boys, what's up?" Stark greeted us as we rounded the corner to the firing range.

"Not much," I answered.

"Is there training today or something, sir?" Brent asked.

Stark laughed, folding his arms across his chest. It was weird to see him like this. He usually wasn't in this kind of a mood. "This is just a fun shoot me and some of the boys are hosting today; it's free to anyone. You guys can feel free to jump in if you would like," he offered us.

I could see a hopeful twinkle in his eyes. "Yeah, sure; that sounds great," I agreed for the both of us.

I could see Grant out of the corner of my eye throw me a confused look, but I ignored it, knowing that this would be a great opportunity to get in good with Stark and all of his loyal followers.

"Excellent. You two go grab your pistols, tac vests, and ranger hats. When you get back, the boys will throw you into the mix," Lieutenant Stark said.

Grant and I each gave him a nod before heading back to our shelters to grab our kits. "Look what you got us into now," Grant complained as we emerged from the path back into the camp.

"Oh come on, man; it won't be that bad," I said, trying to cheer him up.

He let out a disapproving snort. "Yeah, right. I don't even really know anyone there."

"Great chance to make friends," I said, trying to keep a straight face.

"Or enemies," he added.

I laughed, giving him a reassuring pat on the back. "See you in a few, Grant."

"Yep," he grunted as we split ways and headed up the separate paths to retrieve our gear.

"Oh, hey, sweetie. What's up?" Rachel asked me as I came into the den and began gathering up all the stuff I needed for the range.

"Not much. What about you, Cutie?" I asked, glancing over at her.

She was doing her hair and makeup from the reflection of a shattered hand mirror. "I'm going down to the kit-cleaning hut with some of the girls," she told me with a wink.

"That's great," I said, giving her a kiss. I knew I could count on her to get in with them for some information.

She smiled. "Want me to bring your timber wolf down? I'm going to be there all day," she told me.

"Are you sure?" I asked, handing the sniper rifle over to her.

"Yeah, it's no problem."

I gave her a thankful kiss and put the last of the kit I would need for the day in my backpack. "Where are you going?" she asked as I threw on my tac vest and ranger hat and then slung the backpack over my shoulder.

"Just down to the range with Grant," I told her, strapping the 9mm pistol holster to my right leg.

"Oh cool. Yeah, I was wondering why I was hearing shots from the range. Is it just a fun shoot or something?" she asked.

I nodded. "Stark's hosting it. I think it's a recruiting campaign for the NWO," I told her.

She nodded. "You be careful out there, and don't argue with them. They can't be trusted," she reminded me.

I nodded in agreement. "Don't worry about me. I'll be fine," I promised her.

She gave me an unsure smile. I went over to her and gave her a good-bye kiss with a reassuring wink before leaving the den and heading down to the courtyard where I met up with Grant. We went down the path back to the range. It was kind of awkward at first shooting with a whole bunch of people I didn't know, but I could tell that they were putting their best foot forward, so to speak, to make us comfortable around them.

"Holy cow, man, it's a good thing you're my machine gunner," I called over to Grant as I playfully glanced over at his target, which only had three bullet holes around the legs.

"Shut up. It's not like he'd be going anywhere," Grant

called back. We both burst out laughing and unlatched the targets from their holsters.

"Nice shooting," Nick congratulated me.

He was an all right guy—tall, athletic build, always with a great sense of humor. Grant and I had met him earlier in the morning when we returned to the range. Turns out not everyone from the NWO was that bad after all.

"Thanks, man," I said, glancing at my target, which had two bullet holes in the head, a few in the chest, and one in the leg.

Grant, Nick, and I walked back down the range where Stark was waiting. We gathered around him. I glanced around at the unfamiliar faces. I didn't know many of the guys; I'd seen some of them around camp but never really had a conversation with them, because they were always off in their own click.

"I'd like to first start out by thanking you all for coming out today," Stark began. "It's dedicated troops like yourselves—those who take the spare time out of their days to come to these events—who are the backbone of this resistance. Without you, we would be nothing, so for that, I thank you."

A light wave of claps rippled through the crowd. Lieutenant Stark smiled, raising his hands up to signal for everyone to quiet down. "Now, as you all know, there are certain higher-ups who think we should just stay here and rot in this forest," Stark continued. A few people laughed at his private attack on Captain Murphy.

"You know what I think? I think we've done that long enough. The wait is over. It's time for us to take back our lives and everything we've lost to these filthy creatures.

The fiends will pay! *Who's with me?!*" Lieutenant Stark yelled, raising his arm up, rifle held high in the air.

There was an eruption of excited cries around us as everyone threw their weapons up in the air while chanting "Freedom." Some screamed, "NWO for life," over the chanting.

When it was all finished, I glanced back over to Lieutenant Stark. There was a man standing beside him, his arms across his chest. The man had been silent during the whole meeting, but I could tell that he was ready to speak his piece.

He had blond hair and blue eyes, was about six one. I could see that he had that confident look about him—the look of a natural leader whom everyone would follow. "All right, now settle down, settle down," the man called out to us, his voice littered with the rough accent of a Newfoundlander.

"The Bi's and I are going to get a grill going tonight down by the lake. For any of y'all interested bring broads, the wifey, or anyone else y'all would like to bring," he said, dismissing us with a nod.

Everyone broke off and began heading up the path in their own groups. I caught up to Grant. He kind of had a flustered look on his face, like he couldn't believe what he had just seen.

"Didn't expect that, huh?" I asked. The feeling was mutual.

He glanced over to say something, but before he could start, I felt a strong hand grasp my shoulders. I turned around to see who it was, realizing it was the blond man from the meeting. "Hey, Bi's, haven't seen your faces around here," he said.

"Yeah, we just dropped by to see what the NWO was like," I told him, taking the lead in the conversation. I was concerned Grant might mess it up.

"Aw, cool. So what are you guys saying? Going to drop by the barbeque tonight?" he asked.

"Yeah, sounds fun, eh?" I asked Grant, who obediently nodded in agreement.

"That's with out a doubt." Goss said, a smile plastered to his face. "Let's just hope none of those Murphy lovers come down or we might have to dummy them eh bi?"

I nodded in agreement knowing he was testing to see my response. "Sounds good to me, I'm Lance, by the way, and this is Grant." I introduced us, offering my hand.

"Goss," he said, giving my hand a firm shake.

"Goss?" I asked, making sure I had it right while imitating his accent.

"Yeah, but you can call me Gossi. All the boys call me Gossi, and the women call me John," he said.

The three of us laughed. "Right on, boys. I'll catch you at the barbeque later then?" he asked again.

"Yeah, we'll see you down there," Grant and I told him.

He shot us a smile before jogging up the path to catch up with some of his buddies. "He seems like Starks right-hand man," Grant said.

I grunted my agreement. "He's going to be our first target tonight," I muttered.

Grant nodded, holding out his fist to me. I smirked, giving it our usual pound as my mind began racing already planning how we were going to take down the NWO.

# Chapter 9

"So how do I look?" Rachel called over to me that night as we were getting ready to go down and attend the NWO's barbeque by the lake.

I glanced over to her. She had her long, blonde hair done in curls that flowed down her back. Her makeup looked beautiful, and her sports pants/tank top combo was the perfect choice. "Amazing, babe."

"Really?" she asked, shooting me an affectionate smile.

"Mm-hm, you always look amazing," I said.

She giggled and came over to reward me with a kiss. I returned it thankfully as she straightened out my shirt. "Ready to go?" I asked.

"Born ready," she replied.

I laughed, holding her hand as we walked down the rocky path to Grant and Ellie's hut.

"Oh, hey, guys; come in!" Ellie greeted us at the door.

We went in and saw that Brent and Jessie had already arrived. It was a pretty nice hut. Unlike Rachel and me, Ellie and Grant always managed to keep up with the maintenance on the place. Captain Murphy gave it to them when they got together just like he had given me the den when Rachel and I started dating. That's one of the perks to being friends with a higher-up I guess.

"So we need to talk a bit before we do this thing," I told the crew once we got all the small talk out of the way.

They quieted down as I pulled out a piece of paper I had been scribbling on, laying it out on the table for them to see. "Damn, man, it's a good thing you don't plan on being an artist anytime soon," Grant commented as we all huddled around the table.

"Oh, come on; it's not that bad," I muttered.

"It's not that great either," Grant added.

"It's a web diagram," I told him.

He laughed. "Exactly my point. How do you mess up a web diagram?"

I felt myself blushing as I heard Ellie and Rachel giggling in the background. "Fine. You can do one next time, smart ass," I told him.

"At least it won't look like I had a seizure with a crayon in my hand," he shot back. We all laughed before getting back down to business.

"Basically, to catch you guys up," I said, glancing over to Ellie, Rachel, Brent, and Jessie to make sure they were paying attention, "Grant and I attended what appeared to be an NWO recruiting event, the leader obviously being Stark. We suspect that the second in charge is a blond-haired man by the name of Goss, also known as Gossi or John. They have about fifteen to twenty-five loyal supporters. I don't think all of them are fully swayed by Stark and Goss's influence, so we need to focus on figuring out who's just going with it and who is an actual die-hard NWO. We still haven't figured out what it means yet, but that will also be a priority for tonight," I told them, ending my report.

"It stands for the New World Order," Rachel chimed in.

I glanced over to her in surprise as she pulled out her own notepad, I guess to report what she and Ellie had come up with. "From what Ellie and I could gather, they've been forming for about a year now in secrecy. Now they figure they're so strong they don't have to hide it from Captain Murphy," she told us.

"Do you know their motive for forming this rebellion?" I asked her.

She shrugged. "They don't want to share the postwar world with the fiends; the end goal of the NWO is to send them packing back to wherever they came from," Ellie told us.

"But that's impossible. There are nearly as many fiends on Earth from the invasion as there are humans," Brent muttered.

"That is why Captain Murphy wants peace talks. He knows winning is impossible for either side," I explained.

The squad went quiet. "Let's do the best job we can out there tonight. This isn't just a mission; this is Captain Murphy's life on the line. He's always been there for us. Now we need to be there for him. All right?" I asked them solemnly.

"Right," everyone agreed. We got up, blowing out the candles in the hut. As darkness fell outside, we made our way down the forest-covered path to the lake.

The plan was pretty simple. Rachel and I would try to infiltrate the leaders, while Grant and Ellie got information from normal members in order to decipher the hard-core supports from the followers. Brent and Jessie were tasked with guarding Murphy's hut in the event that anything happened. Once we arrived, we parted ways with each other, fanning out to hopefully gather the most information we could without blowing our covers.

It wasn't long before I bumped into someone I recognized in the sea of people. "Hey, Nick, have you seen Goss around?" I asked.

"Yeah, man, he's just over there," Nick told me, pointing behind him.

I squinted through the crowd in the direction he was pointing and spotted Goss sitting on a log, one hand grasping a beer and the other around a girl he was making out with. "Thanks a lot, man. Have a good night," I told him. I wound my way through the crowed until I got to where Goss was sitting.

"Great," I muttered to myself, not wanting to interrupt his make out session with some random chick I'd never seen before.

"Hey, Gossi. What's up, man?" I called to him.

His face emerged around the long blonde hair of the girl, his expression instantly turning into a smile as if he had just seen one of his long-lost buddies. "Hey, man. What's up!" he called back, tapping the chick's butt.

She got off his lap and sat down on the other side of him, taking a sip from her beer. I could see from her body language that she was not impressed; I sent her an apologetic look before returning my attention back to Goss. "So what are you saying, Goss?" I asked him.

"Not a whole lot. You don't have a beer, man?" he asked.

I glanced at my empty hand shaking my head. He leaned over to the other side of the log and grabbed a beer. "Here you go, Bi. You only live once," he said, offering it to me.

"Thanks, man. I owe you," I said, opening it up and clinking the beer with his.

I glanced to where he had reached and noted at least twenty beers laying there. Now I knew for sure he was a big shot; regular soldiers were rationed three beers at events like this. "Nah, man, you don't owe me. Just pay it forward," he told me.

"Huh?" I asked, confused.

"Just pay it forward, meaning do something good for someone else. That's how we work around here," he explained.

"Aw, I see—for sure then," I promised him.

He smiled, glancing back to his girl who gave him a kiss before he returned his gaze back to me. "So where are you from, Bi?" he asked.

"Nova Scotia. I moved down here when I was a kid and grew up around the square in Dublin. What about yourself?" I asked.

"Newfoundland, of course, Bi. Where else would I be from?" he asked playfully as the three of us broke into laughter. "Aw, man, how rude of me. I didn't even introduce you to my girl. Lance, this is Ashley. Ashley, this is Lance."

"Nice to meet you," I told her with a nod of the head.

She smiled back over to me, returning the nod. I could tell that she had thankfully gotten over me interrupting her and Goss. "You got a girl around here?" he asked.

"Yeah, she's around here somewhere," I answered. "I'm sure she will find us."

"How old are you?" I asked him as we sipped on a few more beers while we watched some of the boys clear a circle and begin preparing for a bonfire.

"Twenty. What about yourself?"

"How old do you think I am?" I asked.

"I don't know. Like twenty, twenty-one?" he guessed.

I laughed. "I'm only seventeen," I told him.

He laughed too. "Geez, you're just a baby," he said, handing me another beer as I finished the first.

"Drink up, man. I'll be right back," he said, suddenly distracted.

I glanced over to a tree off to the side of the party and spotted Stark. I caught him tapping his head toward Goss, which I knew all too well meant "come over here right now." I stared at the ground for a moment, gathering my thoughts and wondering about the rest of my guys, hoping they were all right. This was a dangerous game we were playing, possibly even more dangerous than a normal firefight with the fiends. One slight sign of allegiance to Captain Murphy, and we would surely be found the next morning floating facedown in the lake.

I glanced over at Ashley, who was preoccupied with watching the now blazing bonfire they had started in the middle of the beach. Stealthfully, I poured out half of the beer Goss had just given me, not wanting to lose focus on why I was here.

"Oh, there you are. I was looking all over for you," I heard Rachel's voice call to me.

"Really? I was here the whole time," I told her.

"Well, I know that now, silly," she replied with a laugh. She sat down beside me and placed a kiss on my cheek.

"Where are Grant and Ellie?" I asked her.

"They were feeling tired and decided to go home," she told me.

"It's probably for the best," I told her. She smiled, knowing what I meant.

"Sorry about that, Lance. Just had to talk to the boss— you know how it is," Goss told me with a laugh when he returned back to the log.

"No worries," I assured him. "Goss, this is Rachel; Rachel, this is Goss."

They gave each other a smile and shook hands politely. We sat there for a few hours drinking and talking, getting to know each other. Whenever I saw an opportunity, I'd pour out the beer he was giving me. Rachel caught me once and sent me a warning glare, which I ignored.

"Hey, Lance, do you like fishing?" Goss asked.

"Of course," I replied.

He smiled, glancing over to Rachel. "I'm going to take your man for a walk to the other side of the lake to show him my favourite spot if that's okay with you, honey," he told her.

Rachel sent him a smile and nodded her approval. "I'm tired anyway. I'll meet you up at the shelter," Rachel told me with a yawn.

"All right. I'll see you back up there," I agreed, giving her a kiss good night and then getting up and following Goss along the shoreline for five or ten minutes.

"I'm really glad I met you, Lance. We need more guys like you around here," Goss said once we were out of sight of the fire. The sounds of the gathering faded behind us.

"Thanks, man. That means a lot to me," I told him, focusing on the walk and trying not to get tripped up by the tree branches scattered all over the forest floor.

"I mean it, man. You would be great for a leadership role in the NWO," he continued. We finally cleared the tree line onto a large rock overlooking the lake below. "You're a humble guy. That's a great trait about you, man. The only thing is I don't think I could ever trust a man that would pour out free beers," he said, a cold tone taking over his voice.

My heart skipped a few beats as silence enveloped us. I turned to see him with his hand placed against his waste where he had a concealed handgun. I raised my hands slightly with a defeated shrug, knowing this was it for me.

"Come on, man," I pleaded with him as he slowly pulled out the pistol, cocked it, and pointed it at my chest.

"I'm sorry, Lance. I really am. Orders are orders…. I just wish you didn't choose the wrong side. We could have been great together."

"Gossi, come on, Bi." I tried to reason with him while praying for my own life.

"You're a smart guy. You know that there is no way you will ever get rid of the fiends. I mean, for God's sake, they take on human forms. How can you ever exterminate something that looks like you?" I asked him.

He shrugged. "We will find a way," he said confidently.

I shook my head in disbelief. "Stark has you brainwashed, man. Just put down the gun and join us. Murphy's always been there for us. Stark is worried about nothing but himself and rising to power. You're just his puppet," I debated.

"Murphy is nothing but a weak old man who has locked himself into that headquarters hut in fear. He knows his days are numbered," Goss replied.

"So what are you going to do once you kill him, huh?" I asked. "Kill everyone else who doesn't support your cause? Are you really going to kill all those who you've grown up with for one man's dream of revenge on the fiends?"

I saw his gun falter as his weapon kind of lowered, my words hitting him like a pickup truck. "Shut up! Say your good-byes, Lance," he finally told me, regaining his composure as he raised his gun to me.

I sighed, a single tear trickling down my face as I pulled out the necklace I always wore. I unlatched the gold pendant and opened it up to see my sisters one last time.

"What's that?" Goss called over to me.

"My sisters," I sniffled, wiping away one of the tears and straightening up, ready to accept my fate. "My parents are dead.... I was all they had left," I told him.

He stared down at the ground, ashamed. "I'm sorry, man. Mine passed away too," he told me. "If I don't kill you, Lance, they will kill me."

I nodded. "It's fine, man.... Just get it over with," I replied, letting out a final sigh and shaking out the nervousness as I backed up to the edge of the rock.

He glanced over to me and then let out a sigh, shaking his head. "I hope you're a damn good swimmer, Bi."

"Huh?" I asked, but before I knew what was going on, he aimed the weapon into the air and started firing away from me.

"*Go!*" he yelled.

I jolted myself back into reality, turning and running to the edge of the rock and then leaping into the air, flying toward the water. Gunfire erupted around me from the tree line as the sharp hissing sounds of bullets flew past. "*Holy shit!*" I cried as I went plunging into the depths below, swimming as far as I could underwater to the other side.

I finally had to resurface, watching the hail of bullets splashing around me. "*Ouch!*" I screamed as one ripped right through my shoulder.

In a panic, I went to dive back down, taking in a mouth full of water. I came up sputtering. The metallic, tangy taste of my blood was present in the water surrounding me. Taking another breath, I went back beneath the surface, swimming for my life.

The gunfire was still cracking as I reached the other side. I was exhausted; I reached up to grab the ledge when a round went through my hand, exploding the rock I was reaching for. *"Please, someone help me! Help!"* I screamed at the top of my lungs.

I don't know what I expected. I knew there was nothing anyone could do for me; the base was probably under attack, everyone I knew and loved being killed.... The People's Liberation Force as we knew it was shattered, and now there would be nothing between the human race and the fiends except for these radical New World Order rebels.

I reached up again but was denied freedom from the lake's deathly grasp as more rounds flew by, ripping all around me. With one last desperate heave, I tossed my arm to the shore, letting out an inward cry of joy as I grasped onto what felt like a tree's root. I hauled myself out and was hit by a bullet in the ass and then in my right leg. I rolled over onto the dirt in exhaustion, cringing in pain.

I was so tired I wanted to lie there and wait for that one bullet to just end my suffering, but it didn't come. I glanced back across the lake at all the muzzle flashes as the hissing of bullets over top of me grew heavier and heavier. I started thinking about Tina, Kate, and all my friends back at camp, and then I just pictured Rachel looking down at my grave.

There was no way I was going to let myself die, not like this. I summoned what little strength I had left and rolled as fast and far as I could, as if I were on fire. I finally found shelter from the hail of bullets behind a dirt mound. I lay there for a moment, panting in disbelief that I had made. And then I realized the gunfire from across the lake had ceased.

A few minutes later the gunfire erupted again but heading in another direction. I realized it had to be Captains Murphy's men. They were fighting back! I had to get back to camp. It was my only hope, or I was going to bleed out and die. With what little strength I had left, I began crawling toward our camp in the direction of the gunfire.

I knew it was only about three hundred meters away, but it felt like ten miles. The cold night air felt freezing through my soaked clothes. As I dragged myself along the ground, I could feel the grit of dirt in my hands, but I continued to pull myself farther and farther toward the camp. The throbbing pain of my wounds was almost unbearable, but I finally made it to the outskirts of the camp, collapsing at the foot of a guard tower.

"*Lance*!" I heard a voice cry.

It was Brent. He came racing around the corner of an abandoned hut. He dragged me to the building and propped me up against the wooden wall. "Where is everyone?" I yelled over the cracking of gunfire.

"I don't know, man. I can't tell who's who. Everyone is shooting at each other," he yelled back, looking at his hand, which was covered in my blood.

"What the hell happened to you?" he asked.

"It was a trap. That whole party was a trap. They knew who we were and then ambushed me."

"While you were taking a bath?" he asked, confused.

"It doesn't matter!" I snapped out of frustration as I fought to stay conscious.

"I need you to go round everyone up who you know is one of us. Tell them to rendezvous at the east guard tower, right here, and then we will evacuate. Okay?" I ordered him.

Brent nodded, digging into his waistband and retrieving a handgun, which he gave to me along with an extra clip. "If you see any of those filthy traitors, kill them for me, all right?" he asked with a smirk.

I returned the smirk; he gave me a reassuring pat on the shoulder. "Hang in there, man. I'll find you some help." With that being said, he raced across the road to another shack where he disappeared, chased by a hail of bullets.

Not even a minute later Nick from the firing range came running around the corner of the same hut Brent had moments ago. He didn't notice me as he pressed his mag release and the empty mag from his assault rifle tumbled down from his weapon. He glanced down fumbling around for another mag in his tac vest when he spotted me pointing my pistol at him.

"But … no, how are you still alive?" he stammered.

"Magic."

I emptied three shots into his chest. He fell lifelessly, probably dead before he hit the ground. Cringing in pain, I shuffled over to his corpse. I grabbed his AK and loaded a mag into it. I noticed a blue ribbon wrapped around the butt of the weapon.

As I glanced around the corner of the shack and spotted a few rebels, I noticed the blue ribbons wrapped around their weapons and realized that was how they were identifying their own from us. I peeked the rifle around the corner and sprayed at them, hitting one in the leg. The man cried out in surprise and found cover before returning fire.

"What the hell are you doing, Lance?" I heard someone yell over to me.

I could tell it was Tina from the nagging tone in the voice without even looking. Regardless, I glanced back to see her emerge from the edge of the forest behind me. "Just playing around," I called over to her as she reached my side.

"You won't be playing around for long with those wounds," she told me.

I smiled. "Always so caring. So how are you doing, Sis?" I asked, setting down the weapon as I watched Tina quickly crack open the first aid kit and begin sifting through its contents.

"Better than you," she said.

I laughed. "That's a given"

She smiled, pulled out a bottle of peroxide, and wasted no time pouring it on my wounds to prevent infection while simultaneously making me cringe in pain. "Where's Kate?" I asked her anxiously as she began frantically bandaging my wounds up to stop the bleeding.

"She's fine. She's with Rachel, Grant, Ellie, Captain Murphy, and the rest of them," Tina explained.

"Thank God they're all right," I muttered with a sigh of relief.

Others loyal to Captain Murphy began finding their way to the rendezvous point as they defended against the NWO. Finally, to my relief, Captain Murphy, Rachel, Grant, and everyone else arrived.

"Don't worry, my son. You're in good hands now," Captain Murphy promised me, kneeling down beside Tina to inspect my wounds.

I nodded groggily from the loss of blood and glanced

over to Grant and Brent who were hurriedly preparing a stretcher. Kate came over to me. She was saying something, but I couldn't focus anymore; everything began to spin.

I felt the prick of a needle and watched her inject me with morphine. The next thing I knew I was hauled onto the stretcher and whisked away into the forest as we retreated. Shame and embarrassment of our defeat was the only thing that kept us company that night. We walked for days on end, if not weeks.

I couldn't tell anymore, having lost track of time as I drifted in and out of consciousness for the remainder of the journey. The times that I do remember are all just a blur. I had regained consciousness once to see the dull rays of light shining through the branches above before falling unconscious again.

Another time I had awoken to the moonlight. We must have stopped for a rest, because Tina was hunched over checking my bandages. She gave me a reassuring smile. "You're going to be all right, sleepy head," she promised just as I had begun to pass out again.

After what seemed like years, we arrived at our new destination. I woke up the next morning still on the stretcher. Rachel was by my side, stroking my hair. "Where are we?" I whispered. My throat was parched.

"Crystal Lake. We made it," she whispered back with an affectionate twinkle in her eyes.

I couldn't help but smile as she leaned down, making out with me briefly before unscrewing the lid of her canteen and offering me a sip, which I accepted gratefully. "How many made it?" I asked her.

"Ten or fifteen. Junkin died last night," she informed me.

I glanced over at the stretcher beside me. It had a white sheet draped across it. I knew it was covering Junkin's still body. All I could do was let out an unhappy grunt, placing a palm on my head in disbelief. I felt a comforting pat on my belly from Rachel. Junkin was a great guy; he used to play basketball with Grant and me.

"Ugh," I groaned in pain as I struggled to sit up.

"Stop. You're going to hurt yourself, Lance!" Rachel scolded, lying me back down.

"I'm going to kill them," I promised her, angrily glancing back over to the stretcher holding Junkin's body.

"Don't worry. They will pay for this," she promised me, the bitter taste of revenge laced in her words.

# Chapter 10

IT HAD BEEN A week sense we arrived at Crystal Lake. The terrain was much flatter, unlike the sloped hills at our previous camp. I wouldn't say that things were returning back to normal, because they could never go back to how they were, but life was at least becoming routine again.

My wounds were healing nicely all thanks to Rachel who had been looking after me like a mother bear to its cub. "Come on, you lazy sack of bones, time for you to do some physio," Rachel coaxed me playfully. "How are you feeling?" she asked softly while putting on my shoes and tying them up.

"I've seen worse days," I tried to joke.

She smiled. "Good," she whispered affectionately.

I could tell her thoughts were somewhere else, but I didn't pursue the matter. I grunted in pain as she helped me sit up and then got me to my feet, slinging my arm around her neck so I could use her as a crutch. I glanced back at the shanty shelter Rachel had constructed out of pine branches. It looked pretty bad, but it kept the rain off of our heads—well, kind of.

"Hey, Lance, feeling better?" people asked Rachel and I slowly made our way across the new camp to the outdoor medical clinic that had recently been constructed. It was a lot smaller than our last one, but it did the trick for now. There were very few people who were actually fit to work around camp at the moment. "Hey there, big guy," Kate called from her wooden desk, spotting us as she glanced up from some paperwork she was filling out.

"What's up, Sis?" I asked, untangling myself from around Rachel's neck and leaning against the wooden counter Kate was behind.

She smiled with a shrug. "The usual."

Kate came around the counter and then she and Rachel helped me sit down on a makeshift log bench. "So when should I come pick him up?" Rachel asked as Kate took off my shirt and inspected the blood-stained bandages.

"Hmm, probably in like half an hour."

"All right," Rachel replied, giving me a kiss good-bye before heading back to our shelter.

"So how bad is it?" I asked, glancing up to Kate who was rebandaging my shoulder. "They're not that bad. Thankfully, they didn't get infected and seem to be healing at a decent pace as well," she explained to me.

"So when will I be able to fight again?" I asked her.

She hesitated, glancing down at me.

"Come on, Kate. Be honest," I muttered.

She sighed. "I don't know. Two or three weeks maybe? It's hard to tell with these kinds of things."

"Two or three weeks? Are you kidding me?" I asked in disbelief.

"No, I'm certainly not kidding, Lance," she scolded with a warning glare.

"To be honest, two or three weeks is way too early, but

I have Captain Murphy breathing down my neck to get you back on your feet."

I let out an irritated sigh, knowing that she was right. I knew it must be hard on her to write her own brother as medically fit for combat, knowing full well that there was the ever-glooming threat of me not making it back one day. We were both silent as she rewrapped my bandages and threw the bloody ones out.

"Good to go?" I asked as she clipped my last bandage together. Kate nodded, giving me a light kiss on my cheek; I could tell she was upset. "I'll be fine. Don't worry about me." I tried to comfort her.

She wiped away a tear, setting her hands on her hips with a nod. "I know, I just worry, hon. I'll go get Tina for your physio," she told me.

Five minutes later Tina came in, bringing me to a wooden room containing some benches, a mat, and some rocks to act as weights. She ran me through a vast array of exercises, a lot of which I couldn't do.

"Don't worry about finishing them all, Lance. It's only your third day. They will come naturally as you get better," she told me.

I glanced over to the door as it creaked open, and Rachel came in. "Hey," I greeted her.

"How was physio?" she asked.

"It was all right," I muttered, trying to wipe the frustration off my face.

"He did great," Tina chimed in.

I smiled, her words encouraging me. "Don't worry, buddy. You'll be back up on your feet in no time," Rachel added. She sat down beside me, messing up my hair. I shot her a smirk and gave her a kiss. She giggled, returning it.

"All right, all right, that's enough of that. You two love birds need to get a room," Tina called over to us as she packed up her stuff.

We laughed, saying our good-byes, and then Rachel helped me up and back to our shelter. "Thank you," I said as she laid me down on our pile of woven ferns with a blanket across it.

"For what?" she asked.

"Everything," I whispered, staring outside the shelter in embarrassment.

"Don't be, Lance. You know I'll always be there for you no matter what."

I sighed, knowing that she was telling the truth. "How did I get so lucky?" I asked myself aloud.

She giggled softly, wrapping her arms around me as she lay down beside me to cuddle. "The real question is how I got so lucky as to have you as my boyfriend," she whispered, giving me an affectionate kiss on the cheek.

I shrugged with a smirk, returning the affectionate gesture. "I wouldn't call it luck—more like bad luck," I said.

She laughed. "It's still luck, though."

I grunted with a smirk. "Can't wait for this war to be over," I muttered returning my gaze from her back to outside the shelter as I saw some unpromising dark clouds rolling toward us in the sky.

"It will be soon," Rachel promised me. I could hear the confidence in her voice, and I just wished I shared the same feeling.

"How can you be so sure?" I asked, rolling back over to face her.

She giggled with a shrug. "We can't be this unlucky forever. We're going to catch a break sooner or later."

I sent her a half-hearted smile and nodded in agreement. "I wish those rain clouds agreed with you, though," I told her, seeing her glance from me to the changing weather outside.

"Oh, come on," she muttered, her smile fading as she spotted them.

We both laughed. "So let's say the war ended today. What would we do?" I asked her affectionately as the dull drizzle began outside.

"Have the most amazing sex ever," she replied with a laugh.

I smiled, giving her a kiss followed by an affectionate rub on the side.

"Remember when we were younger, and Captain Murphy pulled us into his office to give us the no sex talk?" she asked.

I laughed. "How could I forget? I don't know who it was more awkward for—us or him," I told her.

We were turning red in the face from all the laughter. "Definitely him," Rachel finally said.

As I caught hold of myself, the laughter fading, I couldn't rip my eyes from her. "You're beautiful," I whispered.

"Shut up," she replied with a playful shove.

I laughed, returning it. Silence briefly enveloped us as we listened to the dull pattering of the rain outside. After a while, Rachel decided to carry on the conversation. "If the war ended today, I would want us to move far, far, far away from here," she whispered, a serious tone present in her voice.

"To where?" I asked softly.

"Anywhere we could grow old together and pass on to our children," she said.

"Children?" I asked in surprise. It seemed like every time we played this what-if game the conversations would get more and more serious.

I saw her smile brighten as she gave me a reassuring nod, perching her head up on her elbow to stare down at me. "Wouldn't you love to have children?" she asked dreamily.

I paused for a moment, thinking about it seriously before nodding in agreement. "They cry too much though."

She giggled. "We'll have the kind who don't cry," she promised.

I laughed, giving her a kiss, which she returned before lying back down beside me. "How many would you want?" I asked her quietly.

"As many as you," she whispered back sincerely.

"A hundred?" I asked.

She laughed. "Sure."

We both lay there giggling as we made out for a bit. I glanced outside the shelter before returning my gaze back to Rachel. She smirked, knowing what I wanted.

"It's raining out. No one's going to be around," she whispered, reaching for my hand and running it along her shirt and down to her waste where she let it come to a rest.

I smiled; her approval was all I wanted. Gently, I took off her shirt and pants as she did the same, being careful not to ruin my bandages. Then we began to dry hump. It might not sound like much, but when you're stuck in the forest for years on end where condoms don't grow on trees, it's the best thing you've got next to the real deal.

That's not saying that we couldn't probably scavenge some up on a supply mission, but why take the risk to be killed? Not to mention that Murphy's number one rule was no sex in camp, so if the fiends didn't catch you and kill you, he would. We stopped; Rachel rolled off me panting.

We stared at each other for a moment. "I love you," I whispered.

"Love you more," she whispered back, giving me a kiss.

She giggled with a wink as she unbuckled her bra and took it off, revealing her bare chest to me. I remained silent, resting her across my chest where she laid her head and listened to my heartbeat as I stroked her hair affectionately. We lay there for a good ten or fifteen minutes just staring blankly at the trees surrounding us, which were slowly swaying back and forth as the rain intensified, the wind following suit.

"What are you thinking about?" she asked.

"Hmm?" I asked, staring at her.

"You're quiet," she said.

I shrugged. "Just thinking about the war," I told her, returning my gaze back to the trees, which were still gently swaying back and forth with the wind as if dancing to the beat of the rain.

"What about it?" she asked.

"I wish I was fighting," I muttered.

She briefly went silent, I guess debating how to respond. "It's not always a bad thing to take a step back and catch your breath," she finally told me.

I sighed, nodding before unexpectedly being interrupted by Captain Murphy. "What are you kids doing? … Oh, geesh."

"*Murphy*!" Rachel shouted, covering herself up in her best attempt with her hands.

I laughed as I covered her up with my blanket at the same time Captain Murphy appeared around the corner of our shelter. He looked embarrassed.

"You kids grew up so fast," he muttered.

Rachel and I glanced at each other before cracking up in laughter. "I'm serious," he continued. "Feels like it was just yesterday that you guys would be too shy to even have a conversation with one another; now look at yourselves."

"Well, sir, to be fair, it feels like it was just yesterday that there was color in your hair," I replied playfully.

Captain Murphy laughed, giving his gray hair a self-conscious swipe as he took a seat inside our already cramped shelter. "So I was talking to you sister today," he began. "She tells me you're getting better with each day that goes by."

"Yes, sir," I replied.

He smiled, giving me a firm nod. "Good to hear. We can't win this war without you."

I shot him a humble smile as I felt Rachel cuddle me affectionately. "I wouldn't have recovered nearly as quickly without Rachel by my side, sir," I told him.

"I can see that," he joked with a wink. We all laughed. "Well, I just dropped by to check on you kids," he told us after a few more minutes passed by.

"All right, sir. Have a good one," I called to him as he got up to leave.

Captain Murphy gave us a final nod good-bye and then left. Rachel and I both glanced at each other and then broke into laughter.

"Well, that was awkward," I said. She giggled, cuddling

with me and finally letting rest over come us. I was shaken awake the next morning by Grant. I glanced over at Rachel, who was still snuggled up against me contently snoring.

"What's up?" I asked him groggily.

"I need her for a supply mission," Grant replied with a nod to Rachel.

I glanced back over to her. "How long?" I asked.

"An hour."

"All right, I'll get her up," I promised him.

"Thanks," he said, and we bumped fists good-bye.

I waited a few minutes before gently waking up Rachel. "Hmm?" she grunted, half consciously.

"Time to get up, babe," I whispered.

"Okay," she muttered, cuddling closer to me before falling back asleep.

"Come on, Rachel," I whispered, persistently giving her a rough shake.

"What?" she asked, an irritated tinge in her voice.

"Grant and Ellie need you for a supply mission."

"Fine," She muttered, grumpily sitting up. Her hands went across her bare chest instinctively from the cool morning breeze.

"Here you go, sweetie," I said, offering her bra from last night.

"Thank you," she whispered as she began to wake up, giving me a good morning kiss. "How did you sleep?" she asked as she got her gear on for the upcoming mission.

"Not bad. You were snoring like a pig, though," I joked.

She giggled, giving me a playful punch in protest. "I was not!"

"Yeah, keep telling yourself that, babe."

She laughed and then kissed me. I watched her open up her weapon and inspect it before she went out. It was kind of nerve-racking to see her getting ready for a mission without me. To be honest, it was unbearable for a lack of better words.

"Have you cleaned it recently?" I asked Rachel while watching in silence.

"Huh?" she asked, a confused look spread across her face.

"The weapon," I explained.

"Of course. I did yesterday when you were at physio," she told me.

"All right," I said, letting out a sigh of relief as she put her weapon back together, loaded a magazine, and switched her weapon on safe. "Keep your head down out there, eh?"

She paused, glancing over to me. She must have caught a whiff of my unease. "You're so cute. I will," she promised, giving me another kiss.

"Thanks, babe. It's just a supply mission; there's no need to be a hero out there," I told her.

She nodded obediently. "I'll be fine."

I nodded, giving her bum a pat as she got up to go. "Be back in a jiffy," she called to me, and then just like that, she was gone.

I let out an unsure sigh to myself, wishing I were out there with them. I knew Grant, Jessie, and Brent would be able to handle anything that was thrown at the five of them, but it was weird to have my team out on a mission without me there to make quick decisions. It wasn't soon after I had dozed off that I was startled back awake by the frantic yells of people.

I saw Tina and Kate racing by my shelter, yelling out

instructions to one another. Once I spotted Rachel running toward me, her face covered in tears, I knew the news would be grave. "It's Ellie! It's Ellie!" she kept screaming.

"What happened?" I asked, trying to calm her down while keeping my own cool.

"She was shot!" Rachel cried in a panic. She quickly helped me up to my feet, and we ran as fast as we could to the field hospital. Grant was there, sobbing uncontrollably as he held onto Ellie's limp hand. Blood was pouring from her chest as she gasped for breath after breath.

"Keep breathing, Ellie. Please don't leave me. Please," Grant kept sobbing, but I knew there was nothing my sisters could do to save her as they were frantically bandaging up her body in their best attempt to end the bleeding.

After watching her cling to life for about two more agonizing minutes, Ellie finally gasped for her final breath as her body shuttered. Just like that, it was over. Her hand dropped lifelessly, and her head tilted toward me. Her eyes glazed over with the all too familiar cloudy gaze of death.

"*No!*" Rachel gasped, tears streaming down her face as she covered her mouth to suppress the sounds of her sobbing.

"Grant needs you," I whispered into her ear, hugging her close to my chest for a brief moment and kissing her forehead.

Rachel nodded, obediently going over to Grant's side. She whispered something consoling in his ear. I saw him nod, breaking down as he grasped her close. He cried in disbelief that Ellie was gone. I wiped away a tear that was forcing itself down my cheek as I glanced over to the back where Captain Murphy was standing, arms crossed with an emotionless expression plastered to his face.

Our eyes met briefly before he gave me a nod of his head, summoning me to his side. "I'm sorry for your loss, Lance; no words can describe how much Ellie meant to me. Her death won't be forgotten," he promised me.

"It's not me you need to tell that to, sir," I muttered solemnly.

He nodded, glancing over to Grant, who was still sobbing and clutching Rachel tightly. Tina came from a back room with a white sheet, which she gently draped over Ellie's still body. She then joined Rachel at Grant's side to help consol him.

Ellie's funeral was the next morning. Some of the boys had been generous enough to spend the night preparing the grave. It was a sombre mood as we all stood by the grave watching Grant carry Ellie out to it and setting her inside. Captain Murphy said a few words about what a great soldier she was and how she would be sorely missed. I'm pretty sure watching Ellie's still body being buried was the hardest thing I had ever done.

We passed around a beer, each taking a sip from it and trying to lighten the mood with a few jokes reminiscing about the times we had spent together. That's what she would have wanted. As Grant stood there silently staring at the grave, Captain Murphy came over to his side and whispered something into his ear.

Grant offered him a half-hearted smile and a nod. Murphy returned it, giving him a pat on the back before taking his leave. I watched him his stare returned to grave, tears rolling down his cheeks.

I wanted to go up to him and do something, at least say something, but I knew nothing could bring her back. The crowd slowly began to disperse, leaving Grant and me alone for the first time since the incident. I went over to his side and placed my hand on his shoulder.

He turned around and hugged me, catching me off guard. "I'm sorry, man," I whispered as tears sprang to both our eyes.

"It's my fault; I never should have led them."

"No. Don't say that. There was nothing anyone could do to stop this from happening. Her time was up, man," I tried to console him.

He remained silent a moment before continuing on, "I should have let the senior guys take the lead. If Brent had been leading, none of this would have happened."

Nothing I said would convince him that it wasn't his fault, so I just stood there and patted his back reassuringly as he broke down. "I love you, man," he finally whispered with a sniffle.

"Love you too, man. We're going to work through this thing together, all right?"

He nodded, and then we both left, heading through the dense foliage to camp. It was so depressing to set foot back onto base. Ellie was gone, the laughter of the camp was gone; it was like no one even had the will to fight anymore. I saw it in their eyes the moment that we had retreated from our camp at Lunar Lake.

"How is he?" Rachel asked once I returned back to camp.

"How do you think?"

She remained silent, placing her head against my chest. I put my hand on her back reassuringly. I couldn't imagine what Grant was going through. If roles had been reversed and I had lost Rachel, I don't know what I would have done.

"It really hits home, huh?" Rachel asked.

"Huh?" I muttered, confused.

"When something like this happens," she explained.

I grunted my agreement. "You never think it's going to be you."

She nodded in agreement.

"I couldn't imagine what I would do without you," I told her.

She paused, flicking away her hair to send me a reassuring smile. "I'll always be here for you, Lance."

# CHAPTER 11

WO WEEKS LATER I was ready to return back to the ranks. Thankfully, Captain Murphy had given my squad the two weeks off until I was back in charge. Grant, Brent, Jessie, Rachel, and I were all huddled around a map of the area.

We had a twelve-kilometre presence patrol around the perimeter of our camp. Normally, a simple mission like this wouldn't be a big deal, but after the recent loss of Ellie, we were taking all the stops to ensure that this mission ran smooth as possible.

"So are there any questions?" I asked as I rolled up the map.

I could tell by the look on their faces that we all had the same question. "We'll all come back together—dead or alive. No one gets left behind," I promised them.

They all nodded, kitting up. As we headed out of the safety of the camp, we shook out into a single-file line, navigating ourselves through the unforgiving lands of the Harush Forest. After three gruelling hours, the patrol was complete without a shot even being fired. We nodded to the two men manning the bunker as they waved us in, ending the patrol.

"Good job out there. Enjoy the rest of your day," I said, giving everyone there dismissal.

They all glanced around from person to person, talking among themselves and then splitting off toward their individual shelters. "I'm going to run down and get some water from the lake," I told Rachel. "Could you write up an after-action report for Captain Murphy just stating that it was an uneventful mission?"

"Sure, babe," she replied.

With a sigh of relief, I grabbed the aluminum bowl we used to hold water and headed down to the lake, taking my time in order to give Rachel a chance to write the report, which I dreaded doing at the end of every mission. My literary skills weren't up to par at all.

"All done?" I asked, returning to the shelter with the full bowl of water.

"Yep," she said, handing me the not with the report on it.

"Thanks, babe."

She nodded. "It wasn't like it was hard to do."

"You going to wash up?" I asked her.

She gave me another nod, so we said our good-byes, and then I went down to inform Captain Murphy of our uneventful mission. The camp was filled with new faces. Murphy had sent a messenger with a distress message to all the surrounding camps; it didn't take long for them to respond with a combined thirty-five reinforcements for us.

"Afternoon, sir." I greeted Captain Murphy with a salute as I entered his hut.

"How's it going, my boy? All went well, I assume?" he asked, returning the salute.

I nodded, handing him my after-action report. He accepted it from me, taking a quick glance over it before giving me a satisfied nod. "So are you attending the barbeque tonight?" he asked, folding up the piece of paper and stuffing it in his pocket.

"Yes, sir. Everyone from Foxtrot will be in attendance," I informed him.

"Right on. I have something important to pass on to you."

I gave him a confused look, but he waved it away. "Tonight," he said.

"Yes, sir," I replied, giving him a salute, which he returned before I made my exit.

Rachel greeted me as I returned to the shelter. "Hey, sweetie, what's up?"

"Not much. Murphy's acting weird," I told her, letting out a sigh of relief as I took off my kit.

"Why? What did he say?" she asked.

"He told me that he had something important to pass on to me tonight."

"What do you think it could be?"

"No clue," I muttered with a shrug

Rachel shot me a light smile. "I wouldn't worry about it, hon. You will find out what it is tonight anyway."

I nodded. "I'm not going to stress about it. So what do you want to do?" I asked.

"How about a swim before the barbeque?" she suggested.

"Sounds good."

The sand against my bare feet felt amazing, but the water lapping against my skin felt even better. "Aw yeah, this is the life," I muttered contently as we treaded water just off the shoreline.

Rachel grunted her agreement and gave me a kiss. I gave her a playful splash, which she returned before floating on her back, letting the sun shine on her relaxed figure.

"Race back to shore?" I challenged her a few minutes later.

"You're on." She slipped off her back, swimming over to my side.

"On three?" I asked.

She nodded and began the count. "One, two, *go!*" she yelled, splashing away in front of me as fast as her arms could carry her.

"Hey! You little cheater!" I cried out, chasing after her through the wake.

"Sucker!" She giggled victoriously, raising a hand in triumph as she reached the shore just seconds before I did.

"Screw you," I muttered.

She gave me a kiss, a smirk plastered to her face. "Nice guys finish last. Besides, you're supposed to let your girlfriend win every once in awhile anyway."

I let out a defeated sigh, pulling myself out of the shallows of the water. "Sore loser," she called to me playfully.

"Sore winner," I called back.

She laughed. I knelt down and offered her my hand, which she accepted, allowing me to pull her out of the water. "I love you," she whispered affectionately.

I knew that was her way of apologizing. We were both super competitive, so we each knew how the other one felt after a loss. "Love you more," I whispered back, accepting her apology.

I checked her out as we dried off; she caught me in the act and giggled to herself. "Perv," she called over.

I smiled, sending her back a wink before heading to the camp. The fire that night went well. It was little awkward at first, because there were so many new faces, but after a while, everyone began to mingle with one another.

Captain Murphy found me about an hour into the party and pulled me off to the side to collect firewood. "How are you enjoying the barbeque?" he asked, a casual tone present in his voice.

"Not bad, sir," I told him as I bent down to grab a stick to add to the pile of wood we were cradling.

"Good to hear. Did you get anything to eat?" he asked. I nodded, and he smiled. "How about we take a seat?" he suggested, motioning toward a fallen log we had just come across.

"Sounds good," I replied with a laugh. "So there was something you needed to talk to me about, sir?" I asked, getting right down to business.

"Yes. Yes, there is something I needed to talk to you about," he began. "You know, Lance, trust is a dangerous thing. It's very rare to come across and will bite you in the ass as soon as you turn your back on it. I trusted Lieutenant Stark, and look how far that got me."

I shifted my stare from the ground in front of me to him, surprised that he would ever bring up Stark's name after what had happened back at Lunar Lake. "What I'm trying to say is that I don't want to ever make that mistake again. I'd like you to be my right-hand man from now on," he explained to me.

I felt my heart skip a beat as a result of Captain Murphy's

proposal, but he already probably knew what my answer would be. "It's an honor, sir," I replied hesitantly.

"But?" Captain Murphy asked, reading my expression.

"But I don't think I could ever give up Foxtrot," I told him.

He smiled with an understanding nod. "I already knew you would say that. I just wanted you to know that you were my first choice."

"Thank you, sir."

Murphy gave me a pat on the shoulder. We sat there in silence listening to the laughter of people from the camp accompanied with the noises of the forest's surrounding wildlife.

"It's nice to hear the troops having a good time again. It feels like it has been forever," he told me.

I grunted my agreement, knowing this was leading to something. "The rat followed us here, Lance," Captain Murphy told me.

"Huh? How do you know?" I asked.

"I knew that you were hurt, so I picked the easiest mission I could think of for your squad while you were recovering. They were somehow ambushed not even fifteen minutes away from base. I gave Charlie just as simple of a mission last week, and they have two men lying up in the hospital clinging to life now, ambushed the exact same way," he explained. "These aren't coincidences, Lance; we can't have this much bad luck all the time. Whoever it is was directly involved in Ellie's death along with the countless number of other lives lost due to whatever information he has been passing on to the fiends."

I felt my blood pressure rising. Who in their right

mind would betray the People's Liberation Force for an invading force that was hell-bent on the mass murder and enslavement of the human race? "Any ideas?" I asked him through gritted teeth, trying to keep my anger inward.

"There are only four possible people," Murphy told me. "Tim, Jessie, Luke, or Ryan."

I stared at him in shock. Those were the four people I would have never suspected in my entire life to turn their backs on the resistance. Hell, we were more than a resistance; we had grown to be a family. "Bu … but what? Those four?" I asked flabbergasted.

Captain Murphy nodded. I could see in his eyes that he was convinced it was one of them. I began to object, but he held up his hand, not wanting to hear it. "I know this is hard for you to believe, Lance, but who else would be capable of doing it?"

I remained silent, allowing him to explain his reasoning behind the choices. "Luke and Ryan are complete wild cards; they both came to the camp at separate times less than a year ago with absolutely nothing but the clothes on their backs. Jessie has been around forever but is always silent; you can never tell what he's thinking. And then there's Tim—hotheaded, arrogant, does what he wants, and is always late for everything."

I remained silent, giving his explanations a second to sink in as I mulled over the possibility of someone I knew personally being the rat. "What do you suggest we do to smoke him out, sir?" I asked, deep in thought.

"I'm not quite sure yet. It took me up until last night to come up with enough evidence to point toward one of those four," he told me.

"Sir, might I make a suggestion?" I asked.

"Certainly. I'm all ears," he replied warmly.

"We send out a squad to a position ahead of time and then make up a fake mission at the squad's location and let one of the four get wind of it. If nothing happens, then he is cleared from the list. But if the fiends come to ambush the squad, then we know who the rat is."

I glanced over. To my surprise, he was writing the plan down in a notepad. "That's brilliant," he congratulated me once he was finished.

"Thank you, sir," I replied.

He smiled, giving me a pat on the back. "Shall we go back, my son?" he asked.

"Sounds good, sir," I agreed, getting up with him. We grabbed the wood we had collected before returning back to the party.

"What was that about?" Rachel asked as I returned back to her side a short time later.

"Captain Murphy wanted to promote me to lieutenant," I told her, leaving out the part about finding the snitch. I loved Rachel with all my heart and trusted her 100 percent, but I knew she had one of the biggest mouths out there when it came to gossip. I saw her eyes light up, thinking I had gotten the promotion, but I was quick to douse it. "I turned it down."

"You did what?!" she asked.

I nodded, confirming what she had heard. "There is no way I could let you and the others go out while I sit in some hut all day giving out orders. I'd lose my mind," I explained to her.

The disappointment of my decision was written across her face, but I also knew there was that little spark of happiness in her heart that I was staying with her and the squad. I saw

Brent get pulled aside by Captain Murphy, already knowing what it was for. Rachel rested her head against my chest, and I stroked it, comforted by the flickering bonfire dancing in front of us.

Sure enough, ten minutes later Captain Murphy and Brent emerged from the woods. There was a call for silence after which Captain Murphy got up in front of everyone and announced the promotion of Brent Leclare to lieutenant of India Company. There was a wave of applause that coursed through the crowd.

I smiled to myself, knowing that Brent was the best fit for the job. Soon after the speech, Brent came over to sit with Rachel and me, staring at the bonfire in silence for a second. "Congratulations, sir," I told him with a smirk.

He glanced over to me with a laugh. "I should be saying that to you."

I shook my head. "Nah, you would be my first pick. You deserve it," I replied.

"Thanks," he grunted.

"We will miss you," Rachel called over in an attempt to cheer him up.

He smiled. "I don't know what you kids are going to do without me around."

"We've still got Jessie to look after us," Rachel replied.

I froze for a second. Her words reminded me of my conversation with Murphy. It made me sick to my stomach to even think that there was a possibility of him being involved with Ellie's death.

I put the thought aside, placing a fake smile on my face as Rachel and Brent had a conversation among themselves. "Have you guys seen Grant?" I asked after a few minutes.

"No, not for a while anyway," Brent told me.

I gave Rachel's bum a pat, signalling for her to get off of me, which she did obediently. "I'll meet you up at the camp," I told her.

"Where are you going?" she asked.

"To find Grant," I muttered.

I knew it wouldn't be much of a search, though. I left the party in secret and headed over to where Ellie was buried. It was there that I discovered Grant kneeling beside her grave. The dull rays of the moon overhead were all that lit the small, open field.

He placed a flower at the front of her grave and then just stood there, staring down at it. I gave him a moment of privacy before joining him at the grave. "What's up?" I asked.

"Nothing. Just couldn't handle being around all those people knowing she wasn't there," he told me.

I nodded. "We have an idea who was involved in her death," I told him.

"Who?" Grant asked instantly.

"I can't tell you, man," I muttered

"Huh? What the hell? We've been friends since we were practically kids. Are you kidding me?"

I stayed silent, feeling his stare burning through the side of my face. "All right, man, but I swear to God if you stab me in the back and tell someone, I'll kill you myself," I told him.

"You know me, man; now come on," Grant pleaded.

I knew he was being sincere. "All right, but I'm not saying any names. Basically, there has been someone leaking information to the fiends about our missions. Captain Murphy and I have developed a plan to smoke him out. You've just got to trust me," I said.

"He let the fiends know where we were going the day Ellie was killed?" Grant asked me.

I could tell it was taking everything he had to hold himself back from freaking out. I nodded. His eyes widened. "Why the fuck would anyone betray us?" he practically yelled.

I waved my hand, bringing a finger to my lip "Shhh … calm down, man. We're going to find him, and when we do, he's a dead man."

Grant simply nodded his head. "When you know who it is, you'll tell me?"

I nodded. A smile spread across his face for the first time in a long time. He hugged me close, patting my back to the point where I could barely breathe. "Thank you, man. Find that son of a bitch."

"I will, man," I assured him.

Grant let me go, and I gave him a pat on the back as he said good-bye to Ellie's grave before heading back to the camp.

# Chapter 12

THE NEXT MORNING WAS a miserable, dreary day; dark clouds overhead sent us the ever-present threat of rain. It was, however, the perfect day to start our covert operation in order to flush out the rat. I knocked on Captain Murphy's hut, glancing around to make sure no one had seen me.

Luckily, it was still pretty early in the morning. Captain Murphy answered the door and beckoned me in. I glanced over to the table where Brent was sitting, sipping on a warm cup of coffee.

"Want some?" Captain Murphy offered, handing me a cup.

"Certainly," I replied, taking a seat beside Brent. "So are we ready to get this thing underway?" I asked, taking a sip of the warm coffee before setting the cup on Captain Murphy's desk.

Both men nodded. "Excellent," I muttered.

"So basically the three men of interest are Tim, Ryan, and Luke. They have been in our base less than a year. Since their appearance, these lucky ambushes by the fiends have followed, so in order to find the culprit, we're going to send Foxtrot out tomorrow morning to test Tim."

"Brent, you will pass on the false information to him once Lance and his men are in position. If Tim ends up being clean, then we will pass on fake information to Ryan the next morning and repeat the process for Luke," Captain Murphy explained.

I stared at him confused. "Three, sir?" I asked.

Captain Murphy nodded. I continued to stare at him. There was no way he could have forgotten about Jessie. I decided he must have a reason for not mentioning his name and let it go. I sat in silence as Brent asked a few questions, which Murphy answered. "Any questions for me, Lance?" Murphy asked me.

I shook my head. "Good. All right, you two are dismissed," he told us.

We both saluted before leaving. I was still a bit shaken up. How could Captain Murphy forget about someone who could have been involved with Ellie's death?

"Oh, I forgot. Can I have a moment of your time, Lance?" Captain Murphy called out from the door of his hut as Brent and I headed toward our shelters.

"Yes, sir," I called back, returning to his side.

Brent glanced back at us, probably thinking nothing of it before disappearing around a shelter. Captain Murphy let me back into the hut, answering my confused look with a smile.

"You didn't forget about Jessie did you, sir?" I asked, realizing he had left his name out on purpose.

"Of course not. I chose not to bring his name up, because Jessie and Brent are best friends. If Brent knew his friend was being investigated, he would flip out in his defence," Murphy explained to me.

I nodded, knowing he was speaking the truth. "So what's the plan, sir?" I asked.

"I've already sent Bravo out to the ambush location. I want you to inform Jessie as soon as you can that Bravo has gone out on a four-hour roaming patrol and is likely to take a break for lunch by Pebble Pond," Captain Murphy directed.

I smiled. "Yes, sir," I replied.

He returned the smile, dismissing me. I didn't need to be told twice. I quickly left the hut and walked along the camps outer edge in search of Jessie. After a couple of minutes of looking around, I found him doing laundry by the north guard tower. "Hey, man, what's up?" I called, leaning against the fence we had put up around the camp about three days earlier.

"You're looking at it," Jessie muttered, uninterested by my presence as he continued to hang his clothes up. "We got a mission this morning or something?" he asked, glancing over at me and probably wondering why I was still around given that we didn't usually hang out much outside of work.

"Nah, we're off for the day. I was just going for a walk and letting Rachel sleep in," I said, trying my best to keep my composure.

"Right on. Is anything going on today?" he asked, returning his attention back to the laundry.

I felt myself jump up inside as the window of opportunity opened. "Not really. Joseph took his boys out about half an hour ago for a roaming patrol. They're out for the day from what I hear, probably stopping around Pebble Pond or something for lunch," I told him, casually attempting to plant the seed in his head.

"Joseph from Bravo?" he asked.

"Mm-hm," I grunted.

"Right on. He's a cool cat. I doubt they'll run into any trouble out there," Jessie responded.

"Yeah, I hope your right. Well, anyway, I'll catch you later," I called to him, getting off the fence and sauntering away.

"All right, man. Peace," he called back.

I smiled to myself, knowing he bought the bait. As I walked by Captain Murphy's hut, I spotted him smoking. He gave me a questioning stare, and I returned it with a nod, signalling the job was done.

He smiled, returning the nod before disappearing back into his hut. I returned to my shelter to find that Rachel was still sleeping. I snuck back under the blankets with her and wrapped my arms around her still body, closing my eyes and listening to her soft snores.

She began to stir about half an hour later, rolling over and giving me a kiss good morning. I smiled. "How did you sleep?"

She shrugged. "Not bad. Where were you this morning?"

"Huh?" I asked, my heart skipping a beat, thinking my cover was blown.

"When I woke up this morning, you weren't here," she muttered with a yawn.

"I went for a walk," I lied, quickly covering my tracks.

"At eight o'clock in the morning?" she asked suspiciously.

"I didn't want to wake you up, babe." I gave her a kiss, hoping it would put an end to her suspicions. It seemed to do the trick as she returned the smile and snuggled closer to me.

"No more early morning excursions without me. It's a dangerous world out there," she joked, but I could tell the underlining seriousness behind it.

"Roger that," I replied.

We lounged around under the blankets for a bit, sheltered from the wind that was picking up outside. "Hey, you guys busy?" Grant's voice rang out.

I glanced from under the blanket, seeing Grant standing outside our shelter. "Never too busy for you, buddy. Come on in," I greeted him with a wave.

"Morning, sweetie," Rachel added as he came in and handed us each an apple as he sat down at the end of our makeshift bed.

"Sup," he greeted her, returning the smile.

We had been being extra nice to Grant lately just knowing he was going through a hard time and all. I knew he would do the same if I were ever in his situation. "Anything to do today?" Grant asked through a mouthful of apple.

"Nah, we got the day off," I informed him.

I saw his eyes instantly fill with disappointment. "You can hang out with us, though," Rachel quickly chimed in; she must have spotted it as well.

"Thanks, but I don't feel like being a third wheel," he muttered with a half-hearted smile.

"We don't think of you like that!" I jumped in instantly.

"Yeah, come on, Grant. If anything, you're the missing piece. Lance and I just bicker all day like a married couple when you're not around," Rachel told him.

We all laughed. "You know what we should do?" Grant asked.

I could hear the hint of excitement in his voice. "What?" Rachel replied.

"Rebuild a basketball court," Grant suggested. "Morale around camp would skyrocket through the roof."

"Yeah, that's a sick idea," I agreed, glancing over at Rachel who shot me a smile of approval.

After clearing away rocks and vegetation, we began construction on the basketball court immediately. Rachel busied herself with sweeping the court and patting it down with fresh dirt, while Grant and I worked on the net.

"How's this for a backboard?" Grant called over to me, setting down his saw.

I glanced over at the flat board he had constructed and nodded my approval. "Bring it over here."

He did obediently, handing me the backboard. I took out my hunting knife and carved the square that people should aim for. "Good to go?" I asked, holding it up for him to see.

"Right on," he answered, bringing it over to a suitable log we had found to serve as the basketball net's pole.

Captain Murphy walked by and spotted the three of us busily working. I glanced over to him, wiping the sweat from my eyes. He gave me the thumbs up, which I returned before getting back to work on the net's rim.

"Looks like it's coming along nicely," a voice called from behind us soon after.

I turned to see Brent watching us, hands placed on his hips. "Yeah, slow but steady," I called back to him as Grant and Rachel joined my side for a short break.

"You could always join in, sir," Grant offered playfully.

Brent laughed. "I wish." He held out five nails to me.

"Thanks, man."

He smiled, giving me a nod. "Captain Murphy asked me to get them for you," he explained. I figured he didn't want to take all the credit for the generous offer.

I smiled in appreciation, knowing how thin supplies were around camp. Brent definitely had to do some backdoor deals just to get the nails. "Well, anyway, you guys behave. I've got to get back to work," Brent told us.

The three of us re thanked him, saying our good-byes before returning to the construction of the basketball court. Grant took over making the rim, and I began to dig the hole to support the upright log. About an hour later we were putting the final touches on the small court we had constructed.

I nailed the net together before the three of us muscled it into the hole and covered it up while setting large rocks around the base. "Well done, guys," I congratulated my fellow workers.

The three of us gave high fives all around and joked around for a second. The happiness, however, soon faded as we realized we were missing one key component. "Where the hell are we going to find a basketball?" Rachel muttered.

Grant and I shrugged, hitting a dead end. "You know, Captain Murphy may still have the camp's tournament ball," Grant reminded me.

"Oh yeah, good call," I said.

Every six months at our old camp on Lunar Lake, we would have a basketball tournament. The winners would sign their names on Captain Murphy's basketball, which he kept in his cabin. The three of us walked over to Murphy's hut, bumping into Bravo on the way. The group was returning from their mission.

"Hey, boys, all went well?" I asked.

Joseph nodded. "Not a single shot fired," he told me with a secret smile.

I returned it, thrilled to find out that Jessie wasn't the rat. Once the three of us arrived at Captain Murphy's hut, we spotted him outside. He was sitting in his chair, puffing on a cigarette contently. He smiled at the sight of us approaching.

Murphy reached under his chair and grabbed the already inflated champions' basketball we traditionally used around camp for special events. "I had a feeling you guys would be needing this," he said with a smirk. He tossed the ball, which bounced along the patio of the hut and came to a rest in my hands. "Thank you, sir," we called back.

He smiled, giving us a wave as he returned back to his cigarette. I was surprised to find Jessie at the court inspecting the net as we returned. "Pretty nice job," he told us.

"Yeah, she'll last a few games. Down for one?" Grant asked.

"You know it," he replied.

"Rachel and me versus you two?" I asked.

They nodded, which was all that was needed; the game was instantly sparked.

The next morning's mission was pretty simple. Tim was being put to the test, so my squad had to bush bash for five hours until we reached our squad's ambush position. "Eagle Nest, this is Foxtrot. Message over," I whispered into the headset.

"Eagle Nest, send over," Captain Murphy's voice answered.

"Foxtrot, were at the main objective."

"Roger, Foxtrot, Operation Smoke has commenced. Hold firm at your position," came the reply.

"Roger," I replied, allowing radio silence to set in.

We formed a horseshoe formation around the path we suspected that the fiends would use to ambush my squad if the details of our mission were passed on. The dry summer heat made our mission that much more gruelling as the local mosquitoes zeroed onto our location, making a meal out of my squad while we waited for hours in discomfort. Each hour that passed seeming longer than the last.

Twelve hours later I figured enough was enough. "Eagle Nest, this is Foxtrot. Request permission to pull back to camp," I whispered into the headset.

"Roger, Foxtrot. Clear to terminate Operation Smoke," came the reply.

"Let's go," I whispered to my squad.

We began to get up, shaking out our stiff joints when the sound of branches cracking could be heard heading directly toward us. "Get down!" I called out.

There wasn't enough time, though. A full-grown fiend flanked by six others in human form emerged through the brush not even fifteen meters away from us. There was a split second when everyone froze in shock before the fiend let out a gut-wrenching roar.

"Contact!" I screamed, diving for cover in what little shelter the shrubs and surrounding vegetation provided.

The ground around us seemed to rip apart as bullets hissed back and forth between us and the fiends. I saw a fully grown fiend charge Rachel out of the corner of my eye, but she killed it with three shots to the head before returning to the cover she had found behind a large tree stump.

"Fall back!" I yelled over the deafening sound of gunfire.

I heard the command being passed to everyone before beginning our retreat back to the camp. A bullet zipped right by my head, missing me by inches before finding its mark right into Jessie's back. "Jessie's down!" I yelled over to Rachel and Grant.

They were immediately by our side, protecting him. "Hurry, Lance!" Rachel screamed at me as I fumbled around with untying the stretcher from Jessie's backpack. He let out an agonizing groan.

"Hang on, man. We're going to get you out of here!" I promised as Grant and I got him onto the stretcher.

We began back to camp as fast as humanly possible, Rachel covering our rear with bursts of fire from her submachine gun. The sounds of gunfire faded behind us.

"What happened?" Tina asked urgently as she and Kate came running out of the field hospital to take the stretcher from us.

"He has a single gunshot wound to the back," I told her.

She nodded as the two of them rushed Jessie out of sight to the field hospital. "Hang in there, buddy!" Grant called to him as he was swept away.

I saw his hand rise from the side of the stretcher and signal a thumbs up. Jessie was a strong dude; I knew he would pull through. Rachel began crying into my chest and hugging me closely.

I glanced over to the crowd that had formed and spotted Tim. Our eyes met. He had to have known the jig was up, because he ducked out of sight, scurrying away into the sea of people.

"I'm going to kill him," I muttered.

"Huh?" Rachel asked, staring up at me, a confused expression across her face.

I let her go and headed toward the crowd, Grant close by my side.

"Who's the rat?" he asked, each word laced with anger.

"Tim," I grunted.

"Son of a bitch."

The crowd of PLF soldiers dispersed, realizing something was wrong by the look on our faces. "Whoa, whoa, boys. Let's not act out of anger. Think this through," Captain Murphy ordered us, stepping forward to stop us.

"Too late," Grant muttered.

"It's personal now," I told Murphy.

He took a step back, staring at both of us. With a final sigh, he gave us his nod of approval and stepped out of our way. "Go get him, boys."

Grant and I drew our pistols as we continued heading toward the center of the camp. "Where's Tim?" I shouted to a man passing by.

"He just went in there," the man said, pointing toward the meal hall.

"He knows," Grant told me.

"Watch yourself," I warned him, getting the same vibe.

Sure enough, as we rounded the corner to the meal hall, the window burst open revealing Tim, pistol aimed right at us. I pushed Grant aside as five shots rang out. We returned fire, peppering the place with bullets. Tim retreated behind the wall.

"Reloading!" I yelled over to Grant, sprinting toward the door as I pressed the mag release.

"Covering!" Grant yelled back, firing three more shots into the window.

I set myself up against the wall next to the door. Grant followed suit, giving my arm a squeeze. "*Yaw!*" I yelled kicking in the door.

I was instantly greeted by Tim, who tackled me to the wall and desperately reached for my gun. I fired a shot, which grazed his arm before ricocheting off the floor in front of us. He let out an enraged fiend growl as his eyes turned red.

"Holy shit!" I grunted in surprise.

He knocked me to the floor as Grant fired a shot into his shoulder. That didn't stop him, though. He let out another enraged growl, knocked Grant over sending his firearm flying, and then scampered outside.

Grant and I both recovered our pistols and raced after him. We both emptied our magazines into the air as the fiend disappeared over the trees, but if any of our rounds found their mark, they didn't slow him down.

"Shit," Grant and I both yelled in a mixture of anger and disbelief. I couldn't believe he had escaped.

"And that's why you wait," Captain Murphy's voice called from behind us.

I turned toward him, embarrassed by our failure. "Sorry, sir," I apologized for the both of us.

"Anger is a powerful force, boys. When you act with your heart and not your head, things like this will happen," Captain Murphy explained.

"Yes, sir, we were out of line. It won't happen again," Grant promised.

He gave us a firm nod, accepting our apology.

"So what do we do now?" Grant asked.

"There is nothing to do but sit and wait," Murphy told us.

"But ... they surely have this area marked for their artillery fire," I began in protest.

I was immediately silenced as Murphy raised his hand. "There is nothing we can do. You don't understand our position, Lance. If we retreat any farther, we are giving them the entire valley of the Harush Forest. Our allies all over the region will be cut off right through the middle," Murphy explained.

I could see his mind racing, knowing we were close to defeat. "Go visit Jessie. I'm sure he needs you boys," Murphy ordered us and then left without another word.

Kate was at the main desk when we arrived. "How is he?" I asked, referring to Jessie.

"He's stable." She paused; we could hear the groans of injured soldiers from the other room.

"But?" Grant asked.

She shrugged. "I don't really know how to say this, but he's never going to walk again," she told us.

I felt my heart crawl into my throat, making the next sentence out of my mouth almost incomprehensible. "Does he know?"

Kate nodded. "He's been crying ever since."

Grant and I rounded the corner to where the beds were and spotted Tina and Rachel at Jessie's bedside, consoling him quietly. "You all right?" we asked him.

He sniffed, wiping away tears before clearing his throat. "Looks like I'm out of the squad for a while," he muttered.

I took a seat beside him and gave him a pat on his shoulder "It'll work itself out. Man, they got procedures to help you walk again," I said.

"Yeah, before the war," he grunted.

I remained silent, not knowing what to say. "What was that gunfire about?" he asked, breaking the silence.

"We found a rat in the camp," I told him.

"Who was it?"

"Tim."

Jessie closed his eyes, smashing his fist against the bed. I felt bad for him; I knew they were good friends. "Did you know he was a fiend?" I asked.

The genuine expression of shock that spread across Jessie's face convinced me that he knew nothing without him saying a word. "You killed him?" he asked.

I shook my head. "He got away."

Jessie glanced over to Grant who nodded, confirming my story.

"Don't even worry about that, though. We'll take care of him," I told Jessie.

He nodded about to say something when he was interrupted by Brent who appeared around the corner of the medical ward. "Hey, big guy, what's going on?" he called to Jessie as he grabbed a seat beside us.

It was weird having the five of us there. It was almost like a faint image of what Foxtrot used to be.

"Not much. Looks like I'm out of the war for good," Jessie told him, trying to act tough and keep from breaking down in front of us.

"I heard," Brent muttered apologetically. "Fat chance of me letting you take a sideline, though. You've been reassigned to headquarters with me and Captain Murphy whenever you feel up to it."

"Right on," he replied, offering a faint smile.

There was a wave of small talk that followed as we all gave our best attempt at cheering him up while making sure he was comfortable. An explosion heard off in the distance warranted our attention.

"What was that?" Tina asked.

"Artillery," I muttered.

"Huh?"

"Tim must have given them our location. Now they're going to throw pot shots at us," I explained to her.

We all went silent as the graveness of our situation dawned upon everyone; it was going to be a long night.

# Chapter 13

T HE ARTILLERY WAS RELENTLESS that night. I held on to Rachel tightly. Her body quivered in sync with every explosion that rocked the camp.

"It's going to be all right, babe," I whispered to her. I didn't know if that was the truth, but it was the only thing I could think of saying. Another explosion hit not even a hundred meters away.

I felt Rachel's grip tighten, her knuckles turning white. "I ... I love you, Lance," she whispered.

"Love you too," I whispered back, rubbing her side affectionately in my best attempt to calm her down.

The area went silent for a few minutes as the artillery ceased. "Thank God," she whispered.

Without warning, a deafening explosion hit right behind our shelter. Rachel screamed as a huge gust of wind, accompanied by the deadly slicing sounds of shrapnel, tore through our shelter. I glanced through the huge gash in our shelter and could see that it had obliterated the shelter behind us, killing the two occupants instantly.

"Lance?" Rachel asked.

"What?"

I glanced over to her and noticed she was clutching her stomach. "I'm hit," she whispered in shock.

"Okay … okay, don't move, babe. Let me see," I whispered back, trying to keep her calm.

She cringed and slowly removed her hand from the wound. Blood came gushing out. "Keep pressure on it!" I instructed, hurriedly covering the wound with my hands.

She brought hers over my hands weakly. "I need you to be strong, Rachel. Okay? Can you do that for me?" I asked her as she traded her hands with mine.

Tears were trickling down her face as she gulped, giving me a nod. With one last kiss on the forehead, I got up to my knees and made my way to the medical hut as fast as I could.

"What happened?" Kate called to me as I reached the medical hut.

"It's Rachel. She's hit!" I yelled over the unrelenting explosions of artillery pounding the base.

"This is all I have!" Kate screamed, handing me three field dressings and a white pad to soak the blood.

"Are you kidding me?" I yelled back, staring at the supplies in disbelief.

"We have nothing left!" she yelled, motioning toward the medical ward with her hand.

I glanced through the door; every cot was occupied—soldiers, women, and children who were all covered in shrapnel wounds.

"Jesus," I whispered.

"It's a massacre," she replied.

I looked away. "It's over."

"What's over?" she asked.

"Everything," I whispered before running back toward my shelter, ignoring her calls to come back.

When I returned, Rachel was still conscious. Her chest heaved in and out as she fought to keep pressure on the wound. "Good job, babe. You're doing amazing," I whispered.

When I took her hand off the wound, more blood squirted out, spraying me. Her main artery had been hit. I knew all too well that she would not survive.

A single tear forced its way down my cheek as I bandaged the wound up the best that I could. "All better?" I asked, getting choked up as more tears fought their way down my face.

She nodded, mustering all her strength to raise her hand and wipe away my tears, already knowing her fate. "How long do I have?" she asked.

"You're going to be fine," I whispered.

"Lance … don't lie to me," she replied firmly.

I looked away at the wood line, which had caught on fire, before returning my attention to her. "Not long," I whispered. She gave me an understanding nod. "I love you," I sniffled.

"Love you more," she replied.

Her body shook violently for a second as a shutter passed through her. The color slowly faded from her face. I held her hand tightly, breaking down—unable to hold back my emotions any longer.

"Don't cry, babe. Everything's fine. No one can live forever," she told me, giving my hand a kiss.

It took everything I had to muster a smile.

"I'm sorry that I wasn't always the perfect girl for you,

Lance," she whispered, the light from the burning trees flickering on her face.

"Don't say that. You were nothing but perfect," I replied.

"No, I wasn't, babe. You will find her eventually. I want you to … have lots of children too. Just don't forget me. Okay? Please don't forget me," she begged me, shuttering again as she gasped for another breath.

"I'll never forget you."

Our conversation was interrupted by a massive explosion outside. Her lips thinned as a faint smile spread across her face. "Cuddle one last time?" she asked.

I nodded, rolling her over and wrapping my hands around her quivering body. A few moments later she began gurgling. I held back my tears and hung on to her as she convulsed violently. Then everything went silent.

She gasped in one last breath, which she slowly exhaled before her body came to a rest as whatever life she was clinging to faded away.

I sobbed uncontrollably before getting a grip of myself. Backing away from her, I let the lifeless body of Rachel roll over. She was staring up at the ceiling of the shelter, mouth open.

"Be safe up there, babe," I whispered, closing her mouth and eyes.

She looked so peaceful—just the way I wanted to leave her. Carefully, I reached over her dead body and grabbed her handgun and assault rifle before heading up to Captain Murphy's hut.

"Orders, sir?" I asked emotionlessly.

He stopped scrambling around the hut; a few maps fell

out of his arms. "We need to get the survivors out of here!" he shouted over the explosions outside.

"What about the wounded?" I asked.

"Leave them, son. We can't save them. We're retreating to Hotel Company in the mountains; we can't hold this area any longer. India Company is no more."

I could see how painful it was for him to say the words aloud, but I knew he was right. "I'll round them up, sir," I said obediently.

He gave me a thankful nod as we saluted each other. I made it about a hundred feet from the headquarters when an explosion sounded behind me. I turned to see what was left of headquarters smouldering in flames.

"*Nooooooo!*" I screamed, throwing the assault rifle to the ground. "Give us a fucking chance!"

I held my hand against my head. Everything I knew and loved had been destroyed and stripped away from me. I needed a way out. There was only one that I could think of. Slowly, I felt around. My hand came to a rest on my pistol holster. I drew it, cocking it before staring down the barrel.

"Fuck it. Here I come, Rachel," I muttered. I closed my eyes and placed the barrel of the gun in my mouth.

Something hit my wrist and knocked the gun harmlessly to the ground. I opened my eyes. It was Grant standing there. We stared at each other in silence before throwing our arms around one another.

"They're all dead—Rachel, Murphy, all the others … Everyone's dead," I sobbed.

"Pull yourself together, Lance. We're going to go kill them. The fiends won't get away with this," he said with a firm pat on the back.

I nodded, wiping away what was left of my tears before doing our secret handshake. "One last hurrah?" I asked.

"You know it," he responded, sharing the same smile I now had plastered to my face.

"Raaaaw!" The sounds came from a distance.

Twenty or more fiends came barrelling through the sky, skimming the tree line before landing in camp to finish off the survivors. I picked the assault rifle up off the ground. "This is for you, baby," I whispered.

Grant and I opened fire on them, killing the nearest one as the others took cover. I heard the fearful screams of innocent women and children as they were slaughtered by the fiends, but there was nothing I could do. Slapping another mag into my weapon, I peaked around the corner of the hut I was taking cover behind and came face-to-face with a fiend.

It swung its massive paw at me, destroying the wooden hut wall. I unloaded the entire magazine into it before the fiend succumbed to its wounds and collapsed to the ground.

I couldn't see Grant anymore, but the constant sound of his machine gun indicated that he was doing well.

The window of the hut behind me opened up. Brent fired. "What the hell?!" I yelled, diving to the ground.

I heard the grunt of a fiend that had collapsed behind me and realized Brent had just saved my life. He gave me a wave, which I returned, picking myself up off the ground. I fired a couple wild shots around the corner before making a mad dash across the camp to support Grant.

"Where are they?" I called to him as I reached the hut opposite of the one he was taking shelter behind.

He pointed toward a hut across the dirt path from us.

There were dead women, children, and soldiers scattered along it. I swore under my breath. "Light it up," I ordered him.

He did. There was an angry growl in response, followed by the walls of the hut exploding as the fiend returned fire with a weapon he must have found inside. I sprinted up to the hut in front of the fiend's hut, preparing a grenade while Grant kept fire on the place in an attempt to keep his attention off me. "Frag out," I cried over the gunfire.

The grenade sailed through the air, landing perfectly inside the hut. My satisfied smile instantly turned to horror as the sounds of kids screaming erupted from the window. The explosion rang out, shaking the ground around me.

I bit my lip so hard that it began bleeding. Without thinking, I ran up to the door and ripped it open. Purplish blood was squirting from the fiend's neck. Its last act was to snarl at me as it reached for my weapon.

I emptied three rounds into its head. I glanced around the corner of the hut, confirming my fears when I saw a mother and her two children lying dead in a pool of their own blood, gruesomely torn apart by shrapnel. Instinctively, I puked all over the entrance before my knees buckled, forcing me to take a seat as I sipped from my canteen.

"Shit," Grant muttered spotting the dead bodies as he approached my side.

I nodded in agreement, pouring the water over my head. "I didn't know they were in there."

"They were dead anyway, man. There was nothing we could have done for them. If we didn't kill them, he would have," Grant said, nodding to the fiend.

"I know," I replied, trying to justify the murder to myself.

"Come on. There's still people here that need a leader," he told me, offering his hand.

I took hold of Grant as he helped me back up to my feet. "Let's go," I muttered, shouldering the weapon.

The camp was completely destroyed, but all the fiends who attacked us had been slain as well. There was only one hut still intact—our weapons cache. Thankfully, Kate and Tina emerged from the war-torn field hospital with a few survivors, including Jessie, who was on a stretcher.

Brent and three other soldiers appeared from the rubble, coming to our side. "Is this all that's left?" Grant asked in shock, looking around at the ten of us.

"Unfortunately," Brent muttered.

"What's the plan, sir?" I asked, turning to Brent.

"You tell me, sir," He replied.

"Huh?" I asked, confused.

"It's how Captain Murphy would have wanted it," Brent explained.

"Well," I began, "I think that we should return the favor to the fiends."

"Dublin?" Kate asked.

I nodded. "Not you, though ... You and Tina take the survivors to Hotel Company, okay? You're in charge now."

She gave me a confused stare. "Shouldn't one of us come with you guys in case you're injured?" Kate asked.

"That won't be necessary," I told her. I knew this was the only way to protect Tina and Kate from certain death. Besides, I had no intentions of returning. "You guys should go now. Take the kids to safety," I told my sisters.

"We'll see you guys again, right?" Tina asked, her eyes tearing up.

"Of course," Grant lied, getting me off the hook. "We'll meet you at Hotel Company."

Tina and Kate gave us both an emotional hug. "I'll see you there, Lance," Tina said.

I nodded, giving her a kiss on the forehead before motioning for her to follow Kate. She sniffled and gave me another hug. "Stop being a pest," I joked, giving her an affectionate pat on the back.

She giggled, taking a step back as she wiped her eyes. I gave her a reassuring wink. On the outside, I was acting like everything would be fine. Inside, though, I knew I would never see her again. "Go with them," I whispered to the youngest soldier beside me; he looked to be about fifteen.

He glanced up to me, and I could read the disappointment in his eyes. It was the same disappointment I would have if anyone ever tried to hold me back from getting my revenge on the fiends. "Your fight will come another day," I said. "Keep them safe and lead them to Hotel Company. Inform Captain Underwood that India is no more; Captain Murphy has been killed."

"Yes, sir," he muttered. He then joined the survivors and led them away a few minutes later as they said their final good-byes.

"Time to bury the dead," Brent muttered.

We all nodded, getting right to work. "Can you give me a hand, man?" I asked Grant.

"Yeah, with what?" he asked.

I remained silent. It took him a second to clue in, still probably on a high from the firefight. "Oh! No way!" he exclaimed, shock spreading across his face.

I nodded, solemnly holding back the tears that were trying to fight their way back to my eyes.

"How?" he asked.

"Artillery. She was hit in the stomach. It tore right through her artery," I explained to him.

"I'm so sorry," he whispered as we arrived at our shelter.

We stared at Rachel's still body for a moment. I almost expected her to just roll over and give me her usual welcome. Of course, that never happened.

I couldn't hold the tears back anymore, crying silently to myself as I reached in and picked up her body. I then followed Grant to Ellie's grave. It had only been a few weeks earlier when I could hardly imagine what Grant was going through. Now it had become a sickening reality.

We stopped at the foot of Ellie's grave. I set Rachel down, and then the two of us began digging Rachel's Grave a few feet away. I gave her a final kiss before setting her in the grave and covering it up.

Taking out my knife, I set a rock between their two graves and began carving: Rachel Bailey, October 28, 2018 to June 21, 2037. Ellie Woods, January 18, 2018 to June 7, 2037. Rest in peace to the two greatest girls this world will ever know.

"I don't really know what to say at these kinds of events," I whispered to Grant, embarrassed as we knelt beside their graves.

"Me either," he muttered.

"Let's just remember them for all the good times," I suggested.

He muttered his agreement as he closed his eyes, and that is exactly what we did. "We should go help the others, eh?" he whispered after a few more minutes passed.

I opened my eyes and grunted in agreement. It took

everything within me to tear myself from her grave. By the time we arrived back at camp, everyone was sifting through the ruble of our headquarters in search of Captain Murphy's body. We were accompanied only by the smell of smoke smoldering all around the camp.

I had a rough idea of where he would be; sure enough, less than ten minutes later, I discovered his location. His chest pocket had been blown open, revealing the edge of a brown notebook that caught my eye. I carefully grabbed it, tucking the book in my breast pocket.

I glanced around, making sure I had done it undetected only to spot Grant not even fifteen feet away staring at me. I returned the stare before raising my hand. "Found him," I called out.

Everyone came over, and together we dug Murphy's body out of the ruble. We carried him down to the mass grave of the civilians and soldiers of India Company, burying him at the head of all the others.

"All right, boys; take twenty and reflect on those we've lost before we kit up and go make those monsters pay for what they've done," Brent told us.

We all grunted our agreement before scattering in our separate directions.

"What's the notebook?" Grant asked once we were at a safe distance.

"No clue," I muttered, retrieving the brown journal from my pocket and handing it over to him.

I never really was a good reader. It wasn't something I advertised—not even Rachel had known I was illiterate. "So what is it?" I asked, anxiously watching him flip through the pages.

He shrugged. "Looks like a diary," he muttered, offering me the notebook back.

I waved the offer away, letting him keep it. It would be useless in my possession. "What's the last entry say?" I asked him as we sat down on a fallen tree.

Grant flipped to the last page and cleared his throat before he began reading.

As the days go on, I fear that we are witnessing the last of India Company. So many lives lost for a cause that we will never see accomplished. The worst part is that it's my entire fault. Things were going great; we were holding our ground against the enemy with minimal casualties. If only I didn't lead with an iron fist, the New World Order would have never been formed. We would still be at Lunar Lake, and those men and women who have passed would still be in front of me, willing to lay down their lives in hopes of a future for mankind.

I don't know what else to say. It's hard for a grown man to admit that he was wrong, but I was. The shelling is starting up again, so I may as well direct this last entry toward you boys. Yes, you Lance and Grant. If you're reading this, it appears that my time here on earth has ended, but hopefully yours has just begun. Lead our people with honor and compassion until the day that we can see peace come once again to this world. Never pass a fault and always know that I loved you two like my own.

Captain Murphy

Grant closed the diary; we stared at it for a moment in silence, not knowing what to say.

"Wow," I finally muttered.

"You're telling me," Grant replied.

A few more minutes passed between us. I was so tired from the fight, but I knew it had just begun. The fiends may have drawn first blood, but we would draw the last.

"Lieutenant Brent and the others are probably waiting for us," I reminded Grant.

He nodded. The two us got up and headed back to camp. Grant and I were the last to arrive back to the center of the smoldering camp. We were greeted by Brent, Ryan, and Alex, who gave us a welcoming nod before we headed into our armory loading up an ungodly amount of ammunition.

I stocked up my backpack with five pistol mags, more than five hundred 3.38 rounds for my timber wolf, and an array of explosives, along with a rocket launcher. Grant and I designated the other three to be support. They loaded more than sixty mortar rounds and four antiaircraft rounds, giving us a nod when they were ready.

The hike was long and hard. Typically it would have taken us two or three days, but having never walked with so much weight before, it took the five of us four days before arriving at the outer limits of Dublin just as dusk began to set around us.

Brent, Ryan, and Alex placed the mortar on its bipod and zeroed the sight while I perched myself on the ridge of the hill overlooking the city below. Grant stayed by my side, peering through the binoculars. To the untrained eye, the city would appear to be abandoned, but I knew all too well it was crawling with fiends.

"See them?" Grant muttered.

I nodded, spotting a fiend sniper and his spotter on the roof of a building. "Distance?"

"Eight hundred meters, wind direction northeast," Grant whispered back.

I glanced back at Brent, who gave me the thumbs up. "Clear to engage," I muttered.

"Fire," Grant whispered back.

"Firing," I replied.

The shot rang out, hitting its target dead on and instantly springing the city below to life. I cocked the timber wolf, staring through the sight in search of the spotter, but he had disappeared. The *shwoomp* sound of the mortar as it began firing rocked the ground below us with each round that landed.

I watched the first round land and rip through a gas station below. Brent and the others continued to pound the city with mortars.

"Good luck, boys. See you in the next life," I called to them as Grant and I made our way around the ridge and prepared to insert ourselves into the city.

There was a bang as Brent and the crew fired another mortar into the city. Then, just as planned, they fired off a smoke to cover our run in. "Go!" I yelled.

We leaped to our feet, greeted by a hail of bullets as we sprinted as fast as our feet would carry us down to the nearest building of Dublin, barely making it.

"Jesus Christ!" I yelled over the deafening sounds of bullets as they chopped away at the building's side.

I was leaning against the cold, rough concrete of the three-story building so badly that my arm began to bleed. One of Brent's mortars landed a hundred meters in front of us, hitting the machine gun nest that was keeping us pinned down. We then bolted across the street into a different three-story building unscathed.

"Keep it up, man; don't stop," I called back to Grant, who was sucking wind like it was going out of style.

"Hey, you carry sixty pounds of ammunition," he called back, using the handrail for support as we muscled our way up to the third story.

I kicked in the roof's door and pointed toward the right ledge. "Do your thing," I called to him booby trapping the door with a claymore. Grant jogged over to the ledge, dropping all his kit as he began to tie a harness out of rope. I did the same, knowing our only chance of escape would be to repel.

"Good?" I called over to him.

He shot me back a thumbs up. Peeking over the ledge, I spotted my first victim. He died with one shot.

His buddies dragged him out of sight. Grant began spraying the ground below. "Tank!" he called over to me as the battle waged on.

Grabbing my AT4, I jogged over to where he was extending the weapon to arm it. "Back blast clear?" I asked, peering through the iron sight.

"Clear!" came Grant's response.

I felt the tap on my shoulder just as the tank crept into the iron sight. It noticed us; I could see its barrel swerving up, but I was too fast. One click of the trigger, and the rocket sailed through the air, hitting the tank square on and destroying it.

"Woo-hoo!" we both screamed victoriously.

The tank's hatch opened, revealing flames shooting out as the survivors bailed out. Our victory was short-lived, though, as a single shot followed by a hail of gunfire zipped by our heads. I crawled back to my side, periodically leaning over the side and dropping grenades, picking off fiends as they tried to breach the building.

"Starting to get pretty sporty over here," I yelled to Grant.

"No kidding!" he shouted back.

I glanced over to his side and saw fiends all over the sky flying in our direction. "*Let's bail, Grant!*"

We both ran over to the eastside of the building, which was surprisingly quiet. The sound of the roof door exploding signaled that they had breached. As I balanced on the edge of the roof, tying my safety rope to a metal heat vent, I caught a glimpse of a fiend rounding the corner just as I leaned back.

"Oh shit," I grunted, bounding down the wall of the building at a speed ten times faster than I would ever do.

I was so close to the ground—twenty feet, fifteen, ten. I felt a sudden loss of tension as the rope came tumbling from the roof, following me to the ground below. Before I even had time to realize the rope was no longer attached to the roof, I had crash-landed into a dumpster below. "Ugh," I grunted, feeling Grant's firm grasp on my arm.

"*Let's go!*" he yelled over the gunfire, pulling me out of the dumpster.

We raced down the alley and, briefly out of sight of the enemy. I loaded my sniper and covered Grant, who then put another belt into his machine gun. "Ready?" I asked.

He nodded. We both crept along alley after alley, pausing as fiends raced by frantically searching for us. "In here," I whispered to Grant, motioning him into a side door.

It ended up being a corner store. We decided to take shelter in it for a few hours to let things settle down. As night set in outside, we could see the fiends eventually give up on their hunt for us. They began creating bonfires to huddle around, while some of them fully transformed and flew overhead to keep a watchful eye on the ground below.

The two of us huddled behind the counter with the cash register and stayed out of sight. Grant lit a smoke, which we puffed on in an attempt to calm our nerves. Brent and his team were still popping mortars into the city every now and then.

The unexpected explosions would send Grant and I jumping out of our skin every time one hit. "I wish they would just save themselves and retreat to Hotel Company's camp," I muttered to Grant, offering him the smoke.

He accepted it, taking a puff before speaking. "They'll be fine. Brent's a big boy; he can take care of himself."

"I hope you're right," I replied as he handed me the smoke. I took one final puff before putting it out on my boot.

"So what's the plan now?" Grant asked.

I chuckled to myself. "Same as always—kill as many as we can."

# Chapter 14

A FTER A FEW HOURS of letting things settle outside, Grant and I made our way around to the eastside of Dublin where a group of fiends had gathered to huddle around a lone fire.

"Ready?" I asked, unclipping the grenade from my vest.

Grant unclipped his as well. "Ready," he confirmed.

The two grenades sailed over the cement wall we were taking cover behind, through the air, and landed in the group of fifteen fiends who were getting their orders.

"Lenado!" some of them yelled.

We were rewarded by two explosions followed by the agonizing screams of those who had survived the grenade attack. I got down on my hands and knees, letting Grant up onto my back. He jumped up and peeked over the wall at the chaos.

With one long burst of his machine gun, the screaming was silenced, leaving nothing but an eerie silence in its wake. We jogged away just in time, as fiends came flying to the scene of the attack. Brent's mortar attacks had ceased. I had been happy at the time, hoping they had made their escape, but I now realized it was the only thing pinning the fiends down.

As we made our way through the maze of alleyways, a loud speaker came on, sending a shrill sound coursing through the city. "Come out, you little shits. We have your friends. If you surrender, we will spare there pitiful lives," the fiend on the loud speaker offered us.

"Shit," Grant muttered.

I shared the same feeling of dread. We made our way into the tallest building around, going through the stairwell to the top floor and coming to a rest at a shattered office window. There were three masked men standing on rickety chairs; nooses were draped around their necks. The spectacle was set up in the middle of the street on a stage that must have been used for public executions.

The faces of the prisoners were covered, making it hard to tell if it was real or not. "It could be a bluff," I whispered to Grant. I wished that to be true, but I knew deep down in my heart that it wasn't.

"It could be … or it could be them," he replied in remorse.

I remained silent, not knowing what to say. We had hit a dead end in our attack. It was almost as if the fiends knew we were debating the identity of the men, because three of them walked onto the platform and unmasked the men. Sure enough, it was them. Brent, Ryan, and Louise were left standing there; each stared at the ground in defeat.

"What are we going to do?" Grant asked.

"There's nothing we can do," I muttered.

"But they're still alive!" Brent argued.

I shook my head. "They're dead, and you know it … so do they."

"Well, we can't just leave them there—not like that. They'll be tortured to death," Grant told me.

I grunted my agreement. "What do you suggest?" I asked with a glance back out the window.

Grant nodded toward my timber wolf. I stared down at my weapon, unhappily faced with the hardest decision of my life.

"I know if it were me, I would want someone to end it on my own terms," Grant said.

I stared at the three men in silence before giving him a nod, knowing he was right. No one would want to be tortured to death. I shouldered my rifle and aimed at Louise's heart, preparing for the hardest shot of my life. I could feel the sweat pouring off my forehead as I gulped in a deep breath. I closed my left eye and carefully took aim, not wanting him to feel any pain. I squeezed the trigger, letting out an angry yell of agony as the shot rang out, hitting his heart dead on. Louise's body was rocketed off the chair, his lifeless body swaying back and forth in the wind.

The fiends began yelling to one another, confused by what was going on. I took the next shot, killing Ryan instantly. As my crosshair landed on Brent, I saw him smile, giving me a thankful nod.

I took the shot, ending his life before shifting my attention to the fiends. Grant smashed out the window beside me, spraying his machine gun down at them. They began scattering in different directions as their buddies beside them were mowed down.

"Grant, back out. Pull back to the stairs," I yelled to him as I headed toward the stairwell.

He continued firing. I turned around to yell at him as I reached the stairwell when the wall around us exploded. My ears began ringing painfully. I felt them and realized blood was trickling down the sides of my neck.

I spotted Grant struggling to his feet beneath a pile of debris. We were both covered from head to toe in gray dust.

"I can't hear," he mouthed, pointing to his ears.

I pointed to mine as well and then to the stairwell. He nodded, and we stumbled to them, struggling down completely disorientated. We made our way into the street and found refuge in an apartment building on the outskirts of the city.

"What the hell was that?" Grant asked as we sat down, finally regaining some of our hearing.

"A tank, I think," I replied as we fought the hopeless battle to dust ourselves off.

"We got lucky," he muttered.

I nodded; deep down inside I wished it had just finished me off, though. "It's about time for us to part ways, eh?" I asked him.

"Huh?"

"I don't want the last thing I see to be my best friend dying," I muttered.

He nodded. "One last smoke?"

We shared it in silence. I had a sick feeling in my gut, wishing it didn't have to end this way for us. "Well, I guess that's that," I muttered as Grant put out the smoke.

He gulped. "It was an honor serving with you," he said. I could see the emotions in his eyes.

I nodded. "Same here, bro. See you in the next life, all right?"

We gave each other one last handshake before parting ways. I walked down the street, not really caring what happened anymore. The looming figure of a church began to appear in the distance at the end of the block.

I entered it unnoticed a minute later. It was still completely intact from before the war. Taking a knee at the altar, my eyes raced up the window to the impression of Mary holding Jesus in her arms. I was by no means religious, but I figured it couldn't hurt to ask a higher power that might exist for forgiveness.

"Well, Lord, um ... I don't really know what to say here, but please take care of all my fallen troops and forgive me for those who I have sinned against. I tried to live an honest, peaceful life, but you had different plans for me, so I guess ultimately you will be the judge, Lord. All I'm asking is that you look after my sisters once I'm gone. Amen."

I kissed the pendant around my neck, holding the picture of Kate, Tina, and me before tucking it back into my shirt and getting off my knee. I kicked open a door and discovered the ladder that led to the bell tower above. Climbing it in silence, I heard the sound of Grant's machine gun off in the distance.

There was a heart-stopping explosion, and then Grant's fire ceased. Bats scurried away as I reached the top. I saw the smoke billowing from a building off in the distance. There was no chance of his survival.

"Don't worry, buddy. I'm right behind you," I whispered to myself.

Getting into the prone position under the church's massive bell, I began firing indiscriminately at any and all targets I could find. A few minutes later I heard the sounds of fiends breeching the church door below. I pulled out my pistol and aimed at the ladder.

The fiends' head poked around the corner to the ladder

a second later. I fired; it was a direct hit right through his skull. He was dragged away, and I fired a few more shots down the ladder, making them think twice about climbing up.

I fired a few more shots from the bell tower when a tank appeared around the corner. "Come down, you piece of shit. You're surrounded," a voice called up to me.

"Fuck you," I called back down.

A fiend sprayed up the ladder, making me duck for cover. When I peered back over, I was greeted by a flash bang that sailed right past me into the room of the bell tower. I fumbled for it, but it was too late.

It exploded, a blinding flash filling the room. I gasped for a breath, the wind knocked out of me as memories flew by of Rachel, my sisters, Grant, the resistance, and then, just like that, everything went silent. No more sounds of gunfire, no explosions, no yelling of fiends trying to kill me.

I felt the familiar touch of a female gently running her hand across my cheek. Opening my eyes, I couldn't make out anything but two blurry figures by my side. I sucked in a breath.

It was so painful to breathe. My chest felt like it was burning. I heard the female's voice and realized who it was, but no ... it couldn't be. How was Lara here?

I was dead. I had died on that beach. It couldn't be her.

The blurry figure took a step forward, placing her hand on mine. The familiar touch was unmistakable. It was her; Lara was here, and she had saved me. Planting a kiss on my cheek, her lips thinned as a smile spread across the blurry image of her face.

"Welcome back, Lance."